POPPY'S GARDEN

Look out for more stories
about POPPY and her friends:

MAYA'S SECRET

♥

IZZY'S RIVER

♥

EMILY'S DREAM

POPPY'S GARDEN

HOLLY WEBB

nosy
crow

First published 2014 by Nosy Crow Ltd
The Crow's Nest, 10a Lant Street
London SE1 1QR
www.nosycrow.com

ISBN: 978 0 85763 318 7

Nosy Crow and associated logos are trademarks
and/or registered trademarks of Nosy Crow Ltd

Text © Holly Webb 2014
Cover and inside pattern © Hannah Chapman 2014

A CIP catalogue record for this book is available from the British Library.

Printed and bound in the UK by Clays Ltd, St Ives Plc.
Typeset by Tiger Media Ltd, Bishops Stortford, Hertfordshire

Papers used by Nosy Crow are made from wood grown in

ONE

"I don't care what it is, as long as it gets us out of reading that stupid book," Poppy muttered to Izzy.

"Don't you like it?" Izzy asked, staring at her in surprise. "But you love dogs! You're always talking about Billy, even if you do say he's a dumb blond."

"But the dog in that book isn't like any dog I've ever met. I can't believe we have to do a book review on it for homework. Mr Finlay isn't going to be happy if I say it's a terrible book and I don't believe the author ever had a dog, is he?" Poppy sighed. "Anyway, ssshh, he's coming back."

Their teacher, Mr Finlay, hurried back in from the corridor. "Sorry, everyone! Right, I'm allowed to show you this video now. Mrs Angel's very keen that we all see it at the same time. Big secret up until now!"

Poppy glanced across the table at Emily and Maya,

and raised her eyebrows. It was probably just another mad history project (they were Mr Finlay's speciality) but this was actually starting to sound exciting.

Mr Finlay was fussing with the interactive whiteboard, which wasn't doing what he wanted, but eventually he managed to bring up a YouTube clip and looked round eagerly. "OK, all of you! Watch this carefully…"

The video started with a group of children racing down a patch of grass towards the camera, and then cut to them all digging, jumping in and out of holes, and planting trees.

"This is boring…" Nick muttered from behind Poppy, and Izzy rolled her eyes. Nick and his mates thought anything that didn't involve football or motorbikes was boring. Poppy thought planting trees looked fun, provided she could have a nice hot bath afterwards to get all the mud off. She and Izzy and Maya and Emily had organised a clean-up weekend down by the canal a couple of weeks before, and it had been great. Maybe they could do some tree-planting along there…

"This year, we're looking for a school with big ideas!" A man in wellies stomped towards the camera through the pack of muddy, grinning children. He was vaguely familiar, Poppy thought, although she wasn't quite sure where from. Something on TV? Other people in the class seemed to think so too, and there was a lot of puzzled muttering going on.

"I know who he is!" Izzy squeaked. "My dad watches his gardening show on TV! He's called Cam ... Cam something."

"Morris," Mr Finlay whispered, turning to look at them and giving her a thumbs-up. "Cam Morris. Does a show called *Love Your Patch*."

"Dad loves it," Izzy whispered to Poppy. "He always has to watch it. He says it's useful for work."

Poppy nodded. Izzy's dad was a gardener, so that made sense.

"Ssshhh, girls... Listen!" Mr Finlay pointed at the screen.

Cam Morris was explaining something about a garden competition for schools. "Best of all, if your school's design is chosen, you'll get to be part of our new television series! It's called *Growing Up*. Your school can send in a design for a school garden, and we'll choose six schools to have their gardens built by our team."

"We get to be on TV?" Emily squeaked excitedly.

"Only if we win," Maya pointed out. She didn't

look as excited as everybody else did. Her mum was a singer, a very famous singer called India Kell, so she was quite used to interviews, and photographs, and film crews. She wasn't really keen on being famous at all.

Cam Morris was talking about garden design now, about not being afraid if your ideas seemed silly, or a bit mad, because sometimes they were the best. He finished off by beaming at them, and shouting, "Good luck!" while all the children cheered and waved and jumped up and down like mad things.

Mr Finlay switched off the whiteboard and looked around the class, rubbing his hands enthusiastically. "So, what do you think? You've got two weeks to get your designs in, and Mrs Angel and a group of the teachers will choose the best design to be the entry from our school."

"Just one?" someone asked, and Mr Finlay nodded.

"Yes, I'm afraid it's one entry per school. It's going to be a hard choice."

Jensen, one of Nick's friends, waved his hand in the air. "Do we have to do it? What if we don't want to?"

Some of the other boys sniggered, and Mr Finlay sighed slightly. "No, Jensen, it's entirely up to you. I was going to give you a little time now to talk about the competition, and think about what your design might be. But don't worry. I've got a maths worksheet I've been saving up. You're very welcome to do that, instead of garden design…"

Jensen grinned. They knew Mr Finlay well enough now to understand when he wasn't serious. "I like gardens!" he said quickly, and everyone snorted with laughter. He wouldn't know the name of a plant if it jumped up and bit him, Poppy thought.

She didn't know that much about gardens either, but she did love drawing and designing things. She'd never really thought about a garden design. Except – she smiled to herself – except for when she'd had her princess phase, when she'd been about six. Then she hadn't worn anything if it wasn't pink (she'd compromised with just pink hair bands for school) and spent all her time watching Barbie DVDs and drawing fairy palaces. *They'd* had gardens. But she guessed that Mrs Angel wouldn't want the TV people building a Pegasus landing pad (her big brothers had been very into helicopters at the time, and she'd been a bit mixed up) and pink lemonade fountains. She still quite fancied all the roses, though, just maybe not all pink…

But a garden full of roses wasn't very interesting, was it? Poppy frowned. How could she do a garden design when she had no idea about gardens?

She noticed that Izzy was waving a hand in the air. "Mr Finlay? Where's the garden going to be? I mean, we need to know how big it is, and what shape. So that we can fit the design to the site."

Poppy and the others stared at Izzy admiringly – it was just the sort of sensible question she would ask. No one else had thought of it. But the table of girls behind them were hissing nasty little comments. They knew exactly how loud they needed to be – just loud enough that Izzy would hear, but Mr Finlay and Miss Grace, their teaching assistant, wouldn't.

"She's such a little swot," Ali murmured, and her cronies, Lucy and Elspeth, joined in.

"Sucking up again, Izzy?"

"Ooooh, a project... Lucky Izzy. Isn't it nice she'll have some extra homework."

"It's not as if she ever does anything else," Ali giggled.

Poppy turned round and glared at Ali. Izzy didn't say anything, but Poppy knew she'd heard them. She was hanging her head forward so that her hair covered her face, but that meant her ears were sticking out, and they'd gone bright scarlet.

Ali opened her eyes very wide at Poppy – she had china-blue eyes with long dark lashes, which combined with her thick, wavy brown hair made her look like a particularly sweet sort of doll. Actually, she was one of the nastiest people that Poppy had ever met. It was somehow worse because she looked so nice all the time – well, except when she was sneering, which she did quite a lot. She'd been that way since Reception, and over the last couple of years she'd really started picking on Izzy. Poppy just felt sorry that she hadn't noticed it much until a few weeks before. She would have hated it if Ali had been as mean to her as she was to Izzy.

Izzy just put up with it, and hardly ever spoke to anyone. But ever since she'd been put in a group with Poppy and Emily and Maya to work on a project about Fairtrade, Poppy had started to realise how funny Izzy was, when she was allowed to be. And she was one of the most organised people Poppy had ever met. She even seemed to think in an organised sort of way.

"Shut up!" she hissed back at Ali, who just widened her eyes a bit more. They were practically round now, which made her look even more doll-faced and cute.

"Who, me?" she mouthed, smiling sweetly at Poppy. "Get lost, Poppy. Mind your own business."

All three of them smirked at her, and Poppy turned back, hissing through her teeth with frustration. Why was it that people like Ali could be so mean and always get away with it? It was like she stirred things up to boiling point, and then just stepped away and left everyone else to get into trouble. It all slipped off her shoulders.

"Ignore her. She's a little cow. We all know it," Emily muttered, reaching over to pat Izzy's arm.

Mr Finlay had been fussing with some papers on his desk and hadn't seen what was happening at all, and now he triumphantly waved a bit of paper at them. "Aha! Excellent question, Izzy."

"Yes, *Izzy*, excellent question…" Ali sneered from behind them.

"And the answer is, that scruffy bit of the playground round the back of the Year Six classroom. So if you win, you'll all have a lovely view next year." He consulted his piece of paper. "Oh yes, and the measurements are on the entry form, which needs to be attached to your design when you hand it in, and which I will be handing out to you all now. When I find them. Mmmm. Oh, here they are." Looking

8

rather relieved, he rescued a pile of forms from under their extended-writing books, and began to pass them out. "So, you've got about quarter of an hour to talk over some ideas, before we need to go to the IT suite."

"So, do you think you're going to enter?" Poppy asked Izzy cheerfully. She was pretty sure Izzy was crying, and equally sure that Izzy would hate it if she made a fuss. Poppy quite liked being fussed over if she was upset, but Izzy was one of those people who preferred to be left alone.

"Mmm." Izzy tried to sniff quietly, and the others pretended not to notice. "I might," she added in a bit of snuffly voice, still staring at the table. "I've seen Dad doing designs. It's quite fun. I don't think he's ever done a school garden though." She blew her nose quickly. "His are mostly just people's back gardens. You know. Paths, and a pergola, maybe."

"What's a pergola?" Emily asked, frowning.

"Like a wooden frame you grow plants over. It's nice – you get a sort of living roof. You have them over a patio sometimes, with a table and chairs underneath." Izzy was looking better now. She liked knowing things. Poppy wondered if Emily had asked on purpose, just to cheer her up. She and Izzy hadn't

9

got on all that well at first – Emily hadn't wanted another person added into their little gang – but she'd come round. She and Izzy had bonded over how unfair it was not to be allowed a pet. Izzy's dad said he was out at work all day and it wouldn't be fair, and Emily's mum and dad said they had quite enough children, and they didn't need anyone else to look after.

"A pergola sounds nice." Emily sighed. "Wouldn't last in our garden though. I bet Toby and James would try to climb it. And the plants would just get squashed. Everything Mum plants gets trashed by a football in less than a week. Or Sukie thinks it's funny to pull them up. But Mum's banned her from going in the garden ever since she caught her eating a snail."

"She actually ate it?" Izzy asked, looking up for the first time. She was still a pit pink, and she had a bit of a white-rabbit look about her, with her super-fair hair and her eyes red from crying, but she looked almost normal again now. "She *ate* a snail?"

Emily shrugged. "Think so. There were shelly bits round her mouth. Mum said to look when I changed her nappy, but I couldn't tell. What does a snail look like after it's gone through a two-year-old?"

"Uurggh!" Izzy shook her head. "Shut up, shut up! I can't believe I used to envy you for not being an only child."

Emily laughed. "I'd swap any time. I have to share a bedroom with her. She eats everything. Paper. Felt tips. Bits of her toys." She shrugged. "If I design a garden, it's going to be strictly for girls over seven only."

"You're going to enter, aren't you, Poppy?" Maya asked. "You're so good at art, I bet you've got a really good chance of winning."

Poppy screwed up her nose thoughtfully. "I don't know... The designing bit sounds good, but I'm not really into gardens. I wouldn't know what to put in one."

"You painted all those great flowers underneath the canal bridge though," Maya reminded her. "So you do know a bit."

"I think they were all wild flowers," Poppy explained. "But maybe I could put a wild flower patch into the garden. You know, to attract butterflies. And bees. Aren't bees supposed to be getting endangered now?"

Izzy nodded. "Dad was talking about that. He said no one really knows why, but it's probably to do with people using lots of insecticide to kill greenfly and nasty sorts of bugs. But it kills everything else at the same time. Or it might be a virus, or just that there aren't enough of the right sorts of plants in people's gardens now, and lots more buildings, so just fewer plants anyway. Bee-friendly," she muttered, scribbling a note in her rough book. "No chemicals. Organic. Ooh, and a hedgehog hole! My Wildlife Trust email last week said there's less than a million hedgehogs in this country now."

"A million's quite a lot though." Poppy frowned.

Izzy shook her head. "Not when just sixty years ago there were thirty million of them."

"So is a hedgehog hole like a house for hedgehogs?" Maya asked, smiling. She could imagine a cosy little hedgehog home.

"No. But it would be good to have a house too," Izzy agreed, writing another note. "They like piles of rotting logs to sleep in, and compost heaps. And lots of slugs to eat. Dad reckons there's loads more slugs than there used to be, because there aren't as many hedgehogs to eat them." She looked up at Maya. "The hole's really just a hole. In the fence. They explained it in the email. It's no good having a nice wild flower patch, and the rotting logs and everything, if your garden fence is so big and solid that the hedgehogs can't get in and find them! Everyone has fences and walls now, and there are a lot fewer grassy patches, which used to be like hedgehog roads. They don't like streets, or patios, and I suppose if they have to go on roads they get squashed by cars." Izzy sighed sadly. "I haven't seen a hedgehog for ages, except squashed ones. So the email said to please ask your parents to cut a little hedgehog-sized hole in your fence." Then she laughed. "I asked Dad and he said we didn't need to, the fence is full of holes anyway. He's always out doing other people's gardens; he doesn't get time to do ours."

"I wish it didn't have to be one entry for each person," Poppy said, looking enviously at Izzy's notes. "You know so much about all this stuff. I could draw it, and you could have the ideas."

"Wild flowers was your idea," Izzy reminded her. "And I haven't a clue about what I want my design to look like. I might not even enter – except I probably ought to, just to keep Dad happy."

"Only a week till we have to give them in," Poppy said thoughtfully. "I wonder if Mr Finlay will let us do the designing instead of homework?"

"I wouldn't bet on it," Emily sighed, and the others laughed.

Izzy looked at the entry form that Mr Finlay had handed round. The space for the garden was quite big, but it was a funny shape. Long and thin, and running round a corner as well, so it was almost L-shaped. It wasn't like starting with a nice simple square. Although – maybe that was a good thing. She'd have to be a bit clever, to make the most of the shape… There would be lots of walls, too, so she could add in murals, now that Maya had reminded her about the one in the canal tunnel. That had been really fun. Maybe she could do this, after all…

TWO

Poppy sat curled up on her bed with her drawing pad resting on her knees. She'd been working on different designs for ages, but she hadn't come up with anything she really liked yet. She'd done some really gorgeous drawings for her first idea, which was based on the canal boat that she and the others had ridden on at the end of their big canal clean-up weekend. She'd thought that they could build half a canal boat sticking out of the school wall, and use it for sitting on, with loads of pots and tubs for flowers. But that didn't really solve the problem of the weird L-shaped plot, and it was more about the building than the plants, which she guessed wouldn't be what the judges were looking for.

Poppy flicked through her drawings, frowning a little. It was nice that the design showed the school was quite close to the canal though. Mr Finlay had told them all about it – how the canals were used like roads, for carrying stuff from place to place on the boats. They'd had to do one of his projects on it, plotting the course of a family living on their canal boat. It had definitely been one of their teacher's favourite projects – history and maps together were like his dream come true.

So what else was their area known for, apart from the canal? Poppy frowned. She actually couldn't think of *anything*. Millford was about the most averagely boring town ever. She sighed and turned back to a fresh page. Maybe she should try that grand princessy design she remembered from when she was little? All those roses? A Sleeping Beauty garden! Poppy smiled to herself and started to draw. They could paint the side wall of the school so that it looked like a palace; that would be no problem. And then they'd plant lots of climbing roses. Maybe some ivy – that climbed too, didn't it? Would the budget run to a fountain, even if it didn't have pink lemonade? And… and… Poppy sighed, even more heavily than before.

It was another pretty picture, but it wasn't really a garden design. The only plants she'd put in it were loads of roses and some ivy, if ivy was even the plant she thought it was. No one was going to think much of that. Especially as all the roses would probably flower at the same time, and then there wouldn't be anything else in her garden. And she couldn't see the boys being very keen on it either. The school wasn't going to choose a design that only girls would like.

Poppy frowned to herself. That was another thing – she needed to make sure someone in a wheelchair could get round the garden properly as well. There wasn't anyone at Park Road with a wheelchair at the moment, but there was a little boy in Reception with a walking frame. He'd probably have trouble getting it across grass, or gravel. Poppy made a note in the corner of her drawing and ran her fingers through her hair wearily. She hadn't expected garden designing to be this difficult. There was so much to remember.

Poppy dumped her sketch book on the floor and reached for the essential oils kit on top of her chest of drawers. She needed something to cheer her up and help her concentrate. The oils and their lovely wooden case had been her birthday present from Mum and Dad, and she loved experimenting with them, making special mixtures to solve different problems. Mum said it was one of the best presents she'd ever given anyone, because it meant that Poppy always wanted to massage her shoulders with scented oils. Except that Poppy wished her mum would have something more interesting wrong with her than just being a bit tired, or having had a long day at work. Her mum was a doctor's receptionist, and people quite often shouted at her because they were upset or stressed. Poppy had used up a lot of her jasmine oil on shoulder massages for Mum; it was great for making people feel loved and looked after.

Actually, she could use jasmine now, maybe with a bit of rose. They'd make her feel better, and they were really good for confidence. She might stop feeling so useless at garden design. Poppy picked up the bottles and frowned. It was all very well feeling more confident, but what if they didn't actually make her designs any better? Reluctantly, she put the rose and jasmine back, and picked up the little book that Mum and Dad had given her to go with the oils. She had a feeling that peppermint was supposed to be good when you needed to concentrate. She flicked through the pages. Yes, definitely peppermint. With basil, maybe. Poppy turned over to the basil page and giggled. Yes, she definitely needed enthusiasm, and some help overcoming her doubts.

She dripped the oils into one of the little clay dishes, counting out the drops slowly, with some almond oil as a base. Then she very carefully lit the tealight under her oil burner. Mum hadn't let her have the kit until her tenth birthday, even though Poppy had wanted it for ages before, because she wasn't really happy about Poppy having candles in her room. Alex and Jake's birthday present to her had been a table, a little one from IKEA that was not allowed to have anything on it at all apart from the oil burner, so that there was no chance Poppy could set fire to anything by accident.

Poppy carefully lit the tiny candle, and sighed as she realised that her mum had been at the matches again. Her mum worried about the burner so much that she kept raiding the matchbox, so that Poppy never had more than about three matches, just in case...

Mmmmm... Peppermint and basil was nice. Herby and fresh. Maybe she should do this when there was going to be a spelling test. Or before SATs, next year. Poppy took a deep breath and waited to feel enthusiastic and focused. It would probably take a little while though. She flicked through the essential oils guide, wondering if there were any other combinations she could try. She needed one for brilliant ideas...

Poppy had been going through the book backwards, and now she was back at the introduction. She was about to close the book when she noticed a tiny illustration, buried in the text of the introduction. *A medieval herb garden*, the caption said.

It was beautiful. Like an amazing pattern, all made out of plants. It almost looked like a maze, with the little hedges, but Poppy had a feeling they were too low to hide anyone. They were just there to keep the different sorts of plants separate. But the picture was so little it was hard to tell. She needed a better one, but she was pretty sure there was nothing like that in any of her other books.

Mum liked gardening, though. There was a shelf in the kitchen with recipe books and a few gardening books, and Poppy was sure that one of them was about growing your own fruit and vegetables, and herbs came into it too. She'd seen Mum looking at it when she'd bought a basil plant from the supermarket, trying to work out if there was a way to keep it alive.

Poppy bounced off her bed, pausing for a second to blow out the tealight under the oil burner, because if anyone found out she'd left it burning she'd never be allowed to use it again. Then she raced down the stairs. Their house was quite old and tall and there were a lot of stairs up to her room, which had been an attic once. Mum yelled at her for going too fast, but Poppy loved the feeling of swinging round the banisters.

"Where's the fire?" her mother muttered, looking up from some letters. Billy was flaked out beneath her chair, and Poppy could see that her mum was resting her feet on him – he didn't mind. Then her mum's eyes sharpened. "You haven't set anything on fire, have you? I can smell something funny…"

"It's mint and basil, Mum. It's helping me concentrate, and I blew the candle out before I came down." Poppy rolled her eyes. "Please can I borrow your gardening book? The fruit and vegetable one? It's for school – there's a competition to design a school garden. If we win, we get a TV programme made about us!"

"And you want to grow vegetables?" her mum asked, sounding a bit doubtful as she handed over the book from the shelf by the fridge.

Poppy shook her head. "Not really. I want to read the herbs bit. I found a picture of a medieval herb garden, and I thought I could do an updated one… Oooh, Mum! This book's by Cam Morris! He's the person in charge of the competition. I definitely need to look at this, then I can find out what sort of gardens he likes! Can I take it upstairs?"

Her mum nodded. "Sure. Show me the design when you've done it, won't you, Poppy? I'd really like to see it."

Poppy grinned at her. "It doesn't mean I'm going to be any more into gardening, Mum. I don't want to go and deadhead the roses, or whatever it is you were going to ask."

"Oh, well. It would just be nice if one of you liked gardening." Her mother sighed. "Alex and Jake only go in the garden to play football, or if I blackmail one of them into cutting the grass."

"I like picking the flowers for making things," Poppy reminded her. "Lavender and rose petals and things. I'll look after the book, Mum. Thanks!"

She went slowly back upstairs, leafing through the book. It was full of gorgeous pictures of flowers, and just as she reached her bedroom, she gave a satisfied sigh. There it was. The kitchen garden from a chateau in France, laid out in the same sort of way as the little picture in her essential oils book.

Poppy smiled at the map as she went to sit down on her bed. Somehow it reminded her of her mum's new kitchen tiles. The fancy blue patterned ones she'd had put along the back of the sink. It was the same sort of geometric pattern. Poppy flicked over the page, and there was a photo of part of the garden. Tiny, delicate little hedges, so straight and perfect. It looked like they must trim them with nail scissors and a ruler, she thought. There was a rose bush in the middle of the square, and oddly familiar round green things were planted in between the lines of hedge. Poppy frowned at them, until she realised they were cabbages. Cabbages and roses! She giggled.

She scanned the text by the pictures. It made sense, all the little stone paths, winding in and out of the beds. It meant you could get at the fruit and vegetables easily to harvest them. And the nicest gardens were often in monasteries, where the monks had time to work on looking after the plants carefully, and they only had quite small spaces, so everything had to be planted up close.

Just like the school garden. And it would be easy to make it accessible for wheelchairs, because of the little paths – in fact, some of the beds could be raised up perhaps, so people didn't have to lean down. Poppy twirled her hair round her fingers thoughtfully. She needed to put the green and blue streaks back in, she noticed – they were growing out. She had to be a bit careful with them, because they weren't supposed to have dyed hair at school. But she had really thick, wavy hair, and she only dyed the underneath bits, so she got away with it as long as she was careful tying her hair back for PE.

The monks would have herb gardens too, she read, because the only hospitals at that time were the ones in the monasteries. Poppy blinked. She loved using alternative remedies, but her mum did give her Calpol if she was feeling really awful. It might be a bit scary to have *nothing* but herbs…

Poppy looked at the entry sheet for the school garden and carefully copied the diagram of the real garden space into her sketch book. For a garden like one of those medieval ones, she'd need to be really careful about fitting it into the space – no artistic guessing. Once she'd drawn it out, she chewed the end of her pencil, looking at the space. How was she going to split it up? The monks had sections for different herbs in the hospital gardens, and different kinds of fruit and vegetables in their kitchen gardens. And the beautiful chateau garden seemed to have everything. Vines, even.

Plants that smell nice, she scribbled along the

bottom of the page, thinking of the roses again. And of the way the lavender in their garden smelled so lovely when she brushed past it while she was throwing a ball for Billy. Or when she accidentally threw the ball *into* it, and Billy crashed into the middle of the lavender bush to get it out...

Smell... A scented garden would be lovely. All sorts of different smells. But was that enough? Maybe it ought to be all the senses, Poppy thought, scribbling frantically. Plants with furry leaves. And prickles to stop stupid boys picking them. And they could have herbs that tasted nice too! Mint. That would be good. All the teachers could chew it so they got rid of their disgusting coffee breath after spending break in the staff room. Sight was easy – it would just be hard choosing the most beautiful flowers. But sound? Plants with rattly leaves, somehow? Ferns that rustled when the wind blew through them? Poppy looked doubtfully at her notes. Maybe they could cheat a bit and put some wind chimes in...

"Poppy! Are you still doing homework? You haven't even got ready for bed!"

Poppy blinked up at her mum owlishly. She *was*

quite tired. At some point she'd put the light on, but she didn't quite remember when.

"Is this your garden design?" Her mum sighed. "You sounded very enthusiastic about it at dinner, but I didn't realise you were planning to finish it tonight."

"I wasn't," Poppy murmured, yawning. "It was just hard to stop, once I got going on it. It's fun." She held the sketch book out to her mum a little nervously. Her mum loved being in the garden. It would be awful if she took one look at Poppy's design and said it was horrible, or that it just wouldn't work.

"Oh, Poppy, this is really pretty," her mum said, smiling. "It reminds me of something…"

"Your kitchen tiles," Poppy said, with another massive yawn.

"Yes! A sort of Moroccan pattern. But it's based on a medieval garden, I can see that. It's lovely."

"There's a wild flower patch," Poppy called to her as she went to the bathroom to brush her teeth. "To attract butterflies. And I thought that could be in a butterfly-shaped bit of hedge. That bit took ages, trying to make it look properly like a butterfly. Do you think you can make hedges grow in shapes like that?"

Her mum looked round the bathroom door. "I'm sure you can. Think of topiary. You know, when they make hedges into statues? Like Mr Simpson's peacock hedge down the road."

"Oooh!" Poppy bounded out of the bathroom. "Topiary! I haven't got any of that. That would work brilliantly in the sight bit."

"Not now!" her mother said sternly. "Bed. I know you, you'll be drawing it at the breakfast table tomorrow. Well, you can just get some sleep in first."

"Wow!" Izzy peered at Poppy's intricate design.

"Do you think it's OK?" Poppy asked her anxiously.

She hadn't wanted to get the design out until they were in the classroom, in case it got rained on. It was spitting a bit, but it had to be tipping it down before Mrs Angel, the head, would let anyone into school early.

"It's beautiful. It's so detailed, Poppy. It must have taken hours."

"Yeah, it's lucky we only had that little bit of science homework last night. I did that in the car on the way to school," Poppy admitted with a yawn. She was really tired. She'd been so excited about her design and all the ideas that she'd taken ages to get to sleep, and then she'd dreamed about princesses and unicorns wandering through her garden. The unicorns kept bumping into the wind chimes.

Izzy tried not to look disapproving, and almost managed. She was one of those people who couldn't not do homework. Like she couldn't write the date at the top of her work without drawing a line under it. With a ruler. But Poppy loved her anyway.

"Have you brought yours in?" she asked.

Izzy shook her head. "Not finished. But don't worry, Poppy, it's not going to be any competition for that! And I've seen Lara's…"

Poppy rolled her eyes. "Did it involve a pony, by any chance?"

Izzy nodded, grinning. "A pony-shaped flower bed *and* an actual pony…" She giggled. "Well, horse manure is very good for your garden. But it didn't really have anything else in it, except a carrot bed."

Poppy frowned. "Oh, of course! For feeding carrots to the pony."

"Uh-huh."

Maya and Emily came in and dumped their bags. "Oh, Poppy! Look, Ems, it's beautiful!" Maya squeaked. "OK, I'm definitely not entering. No point."

Emily put an arm round Poppy and hugged her.

"That beats Nick's design," she whispered, nodding to the noisy table of boys behind them. "He was waving it about on the bus, wasn't he, Maya?"

"Yup, and it's basically a skate park. With a tree in the middle."

"You didn't draw that."

Poppy snatched up her design in a hurry and looked round at Ali and Lucy and Elspeth. They were such good sneaker-uppers, she hadn't seen them at all. "Yes, I did," she said stubbornly. Ali had a piece of paper in a smart see-through pink folder, and she snatched it behind her back as she saw Poppy looking at it.

"No copying!" she snapped.

"I don't want to copy yours…" Poppy started to protest.

Ali smirked. "You don't need to, do you. You already copied that one."

Poppy shook her head. "No, I didn't, I drew it."

"I bet she copied it straight out of a book," Elspeth said. "Don't you think so, Ali?"

"Of course she did," Ali said scornfully. "No way she came up with that by herself. She cheated."

"I didn't copy," Poppy said faintly, but she was starting to wonder. How much had she copied her design out of Cam Morris's book? Maybe she *was* cheating. She stared down at her beautiful design, her eyes troubled, and Ali smirked at her two sidekicks.

"See? Look at her. She's gone all red. You're such a cheat, Poppy. Mr Finlay's going to be *so* disappointed."

She'd copied the way the little hedges surrounded the flowers from those photos in the book, Poppy realised. And it was a book by Cam Morris – he'd recognise it, wouldn't he? So even if she won the competition at school, when all the different schools sent their designs in, he'd spot it at once.

Poppy stuffed the drawing into her bag, crumpling it a little. She didn't care any more. She couldn't give it in now. She felt her eyes burning, and bit hard into her bottom lip. No way was she going to let Ali see her cry. But she felt so stupid. She'd been really, really proud of her design, and she hadn't even thought that it was copied.

"Don't listen to her," Izzy hissed as Mr Finlay came in and started to do the register. "Poppy, you know how horrible she is. It's a brilliant design."

Poppy sniffed and put her pencil case back in her rucksack on top of her entry form. She didn't even want to be able to see it.

THREE

"Poppy, are you OK?" Izzy asked her anxiously as soon as the bell rang for break. Poppy had been working silently all morning. She managed a tight little smile a couple of times when Izzy nudged her, looking worried, but she hadn't wanted to talk. She was too disappointed, and angry with herself. She'd felt so pleased with the way her design had come out. It had looked really professional, and her mum and dad had been so impressed with it. Even Jake and Alex had grunted at it in an approving sort of way, in between shovelling in half a packet of cornflakes each. All that effort had been for nothing, and there was no way she could come up with another design. There was time enough, but she just didn't want to. She couldn't face starting all over again. And anyway, she didn't have any more ideas.

She tried to smile at Izzy again, but it didn't

work very well. She could tell she didn't look very convincing, and Izzy stared at her anxiously.

"You mustn't listen to Ali. Seriously, Poppy. I don't believe you copied it. You wouldn't do that." Izzy glared at Ali and Elspeth and Lucy, who were huddled at their table, making admiring noises over Ali's garden design.

"But I sort of did," Poppy told her miserably. "I didn't think of it that way until she said it, but I did – I got the idea out of one of my books on essential oils, and then I added bits to it from another book. So I did copy it..." She sank her chin on to her hands. Talking about it made her want to cry, and she blinked fiercely at the table.

"That doesn't mean you copied it!" Izzy hissed crossly.

"She's right, Poppy." Maya nodded decidedly. "Show it to us again."

Poppy shook her head. She didn't even want to see it.

"Please!"

"I don't want to!" Poppy gasped, grabbing the piece of paper out of her bag and jumping up from her chair. As she went past Mr Finlay's desk she shoved the design into the bin – it was the wrong one, not the recycling bin, but she didn't care. Maya could tell her off about it later. She hurried out into the corridor, wondering where to go. She didn't want to have to talk to anybody right now.

"Poppy!" Someone was calling her but Poppy darted off down the corridor. It didn't matter where she went. She needed to get away from everybody. Why couldn't they just leave her alone? She didn't want them laughing at her for being so stupid.

The library! She'd go and hide in there. Poppy hurried in and grabbed a book off the first shelf she passed. A nice big one. She could hide behind that, and even if Izzy and the others came looking for her, they wouldn't know she was there.

Unfortunately, the book was extremely boring. All about aeroplanes, with lots of diagrams of how jets worked and things like that. It didn't distract Poppy from how miserable she was at all, but she couldn't seem to find the energy to get up and change it for something she'd like. She just stared at it grimly, and tried not to remember the triumphant look on Ali's face. She knew that Izzy and Maya and Emily would probably be really sweet about it if she went back, even though she'd snapped at them and run off. But they'd think she was so silly. (Because she was.) She couldn't bear the thought of them being all sympathetic and nice.

Eventually, after what felt like hours of staring at a jet fighter, the bell rang and Poppy reluctantly uncurled herself from her position on the window sill. She stuffed the book back on to the shelf and hurried to her classroom, her head down, trying to hide behind her hair like Izzy did. She wasn't used to trying to hide from people. Ali and her gang were nasty to her sometimes, but just the same way they were mean to everybody. (Except Maya, now that they'd discovered her mum was a celebrity.) Usually Poppy could just shrug it off, or give as good as she got.

She glanced sideways at Izzy and Emily and Maya as she got to their table, hoping they weren't annoyed with her. She smiled faintly at Izzy, thinking she ought to say sorry for running off. But Izzy gave her a weird look and then stared at the whiteboard, as though she didn't want to talk to her. Poppy stood there for a second with her mouth half open, ready to say she hadn't meant to be rude.

There was no one to say it to. Emily and Maya were staring at the whiteboard too, and Poppy shut her mouth quickly and slid into her seat, feeling about

34

ten times worse, even though five minutes before she wouldn't have thought that was possible.

At lunchtime, all of them went to the dining hall together as usual. Izzy asked Poppy what she'd got in her sandwiches – she was known for having weird things sometimes – and Poppy said only cheese, but she did have lavender-flavoured biscuits that she and her mum had made, which Izzy cheerfully told her sounded disgusting. So that was pretty normal. But no one mentioned garden designs at all, and there kept being odd little silences. Once she saw Emily giving Izzy a funny look when they thought she was busy finding something in her lunchbox.

Maybe they were all annoyed with her and they were pretending not to be, Poppy thought unhappily. Maybe they hated her for cheating. She hardly ate any of her lunch – even the lavender biscuits, which she usually loved, tasted all dry and dusty. She pushed them back into her lunchbox, crumbled into little bits.

"Umm, Poppy?" Izzy was staring at her.

Poppy blinked. "Yes?" She hadn't been listening. It looked like Izzy had been talking to her, and she'd missed whatever she said. "Sorry, I was thinking…"

"We're— Er—" Izzy swallowed and looked nervous.

"Just going to do something for Miss Grace," Emily put in firmly. "See you after lunch."

Poppy gaped after the three of them as they hurried away. She definitely had upset them then. It was obvious that Emily had made up the thing about Miss Grace. Poppy hadn't been paying much attention that morning, but she'd have seen it if their classroom assistant had asked the others to do something. She'd have asked all four of them, anyway. She knew they always hung around together.

Until now, clearly. Poppy swallowed, and pretended to eat a bit of biscuit, so no one would think she'd been abandoned. Then slowly, trying to look unconcerned, she got up, and put her lunchbox away in the class storage box. What was she going to do now? If she went out to the playground, she couldn't just wander about on her own. But no one was likely to invite her to join in a game. And to be honest, she didn't feel like it anyway. She'd have to go back to the library, she decided miserably. Then she gave a little sniff of laughter. She could go and read the book on aeroplanes again.

Emily and Maya and even Izzy were still acting weird when Poppy crept back into the classroom after lunch. Their school librarian, Mrs Peters, was really nice when you wanted to ask her something about books, but she was a monster if people were noisy. She only worked part-time, but on days when she was in the library, everyone had to be silent or she'd just throw people out. And she wouldn't let them borrow the book they'd been looking at either. After a whole break and lunchtime being silent, Poppy felt weird, as though she couldn't have spoken louder than a whisper if she'd wanted to. And she didn't, much. Especially when Izzy and the others kept giving each other conspiratorial looks, and smirking, and nudging each other.

What she actually felt like was walking out of the classroom and going home. Except there wouldn't be anyone there. Mum and Dad would both be at work, and Jake and Alex would be at school. She had to get all the way through afternoon school before she could go home and find the right essential oils for dealing with a really mean group of ex-friends who were laughing at her behind her back. She had a feeling she might have to make that one up for herself. It probably wasn't going to be in the book.

By the end of the afternoon, Poppy was feeling desperate. Izzy had tried to be nice to her a couple of times, but Poppy was already so confused and upset that she didn't know what to say, and Izzy started frowning at her and looking just as confused as she was.

What was going on?

Maya and Emily had to rush off to catch their bus, but Izzy's dad was picking her up so she hung around, trying to talk to Poppy while they put their things away.

"Poppy, are you still upset about what Ali said?" Izzy crouched down and tried to peer up at her, as Poppy had her head ducked. "Honestly! She's so horrible, you know that! You're always telling me just to ignore her. Please don't let her get to you."

It isn't her! It's all of you! Poppy wanted to wail, but she couldn't face it. "I've got to go," she muttered. "After-school club." And she grabbed her bag, racing out into the corridor and making for the main hall, where after-school club was set up.

Except she wasn't going to after-school club, she decided as she got halfway down the corridor. She couldn't stand all the lovely, fussy ladies who ran it right now. They wouldn't let her get away with sitting in a corner being miserable, like she wanted to. They'd be trying to cheer her up. Telling her to come and join in with the others and play a game, or something.

Poppy darted into the girls' loos and took a deep, panicked breath. What would happen if she just didn't turn up? Probably no one would notice for a while. Then they'd think she'd been away that day and no one had told them. That happened quite often; the after-school club staff were always complaining about it. Someone would go to the office eventually, and make sure. But she had a while before that happened.

She turned back the way she'd come and headed out towards the school gate. She didn't go to after-school club every day, so the staff who were seeing their classes off wouldn't notice anything unusual. Mr Finlay was there, but he was "having a word" with Jensen's dad about Jensen and Nick throwing wet paper towels at the ceiling in the girls' loos, so she could just hurry past. As long as she looked like she was heading for her mum's car, no one would say anything. Poppy pasted a smile on to her face, pretended to wave at someone and just walked down the street towards the shops, and no one stopped her.

She'd never been in Millford on her own before. Her mum and dad weren't really fussy and over-protective – they let her take Billy out for walks on her own, provided she took a mobile with her and she promised to be back by a certain time. But there was no way they'd let her go wandering around the town on her own. Mum had said once she was in Year Six they'd think about it. If she went with some of her friends, maybe.

Poppy sniffed and stared miserably into the window of one of her favourite shops, the health food shop that sold the essential oils she liked. She couldn't really go in. She didn't have any money to buy anything, for a start. And Fran, who ran the shop, would recognise her, and she'd know that Poppy wasn't supposed to be wandering round town. Poppy wasn't sure she could pull off pretending that her mum was just in the bookshop, or something. Besides, she didn't like the idea of lying to Fran.

"Poppy!"

Poppy whirled round, her heart thumping anxiously. "Izzy!"

Izzy was standing there with her dad. She looked worried, and her dad looked surprised, and a bit confused.

"Why aren't you in after-school club?" Izzy demanded. "Did your mum come and pick you up early? Did they call her because you were all upset? Poppy, please tell me what's wrong." She looked so worried that Poppy couldn't help wondering if she'd made a mistake. If Izzy *hadn't* been laughing at her behind her back earlier on. If she had been, wouldn't she have understood why Poppy was upset? She wouldn't be looking so confused now, would she?

Izzy looked round, as though she was searching for something, and then she suddenly gasped. "Poppy, where's your mum? She's not here, is she? Did you just walk out of after-school club?"

"Hang on," Izzy's dad said, frowning. "Poppy, sweetheart. Is that right? Does anyone know you're here on your own?"

Poppy shook her head slowly, and then gave a massive sniff and started to cry.

Izzy's dad looked a bit panicked, as though he wasn't sure what to do with a crying person, and he patted her shoulder awkwardly. Izzy gave her a hug, and all of a sudden Poppy decided that she couldn't possibly have meant to be mean to her all afternoon. It wasn't the hug of a two-faced sort of person at all. And Izzy had never been like that anyway. She was incredibly honest. Absolutely the worst liar ever, and terrible at keeping secrets. Poppy gulped and sniffed again, suddenly feeling very tired. If only she'd got more sleep last night, all this might not have seemed so important, she realised. But it didn't mean she could stop crying.

Izzy's dad was leading them into the nice little coffee shop where Mum took her for hot chocolate sometimes, and once he'd got them sat down he told Izzy to order them both a drink, and pulled his mobile out of his pocket.

"Are you calling my mum?" Poppy said, although she wasn't totally sure anyone understood her – it came out as gulps.

"I have to call your mum, Poppy," he told her gently. "I don't know if the school will have told her yet – they might not have realised that you've gone. But if they have – well, if Izzy had disappeared, I know how worried I'd be."

"She'll be so cross!" Poppy wailed, and Izzy hugged her again.

"Dad will tell her there's something wrong. He won't let her be cross with you."

Izzy's dad nodded grimly, as though he thought that might be difficult, and tapped at his phone, clearly finding Poppy's mum's number.

Poppy could only hear his side of the phone call, but she could guess what her mum was saying. The school hadn't called her yet, and she was worried, but not frantic.

"Yes, she's obviously upset about something but she's fine. Not hurt or anything, are you, Poppy?"

Poppy shook her head.

"Are you still at work? Do you want me to take her home with us? I can do tea for them both if you like?"

Izzy nodded eagerly, and Poppy felt slightly better. She had got things mixed up somehow, she must have done.

"Here, talk to your mum for a minute, Poppy. She needs to know you're OK."

Poppy nodded and took the phone.

"Poppy, what's happening? I can't believe you walked out of school like that!"

"I'm sorry," Poppy whispered. "Stuff was going on…" She didn't want to tell her mum that she'd thought Izzy was being mean to her. Especially now she was thinking she might have got it all wrong. And she really wanted to go back to Izzy's house, and try and find out why they'd all been so odd that afternoon. "Ali told me my design for the school garden was all copied and I was a cheat," she explained. It was totally true, even if it wasn't why she'd actually sneaked out of school.

"That girl!" her mum snarled. "Right. Well, I shall be ringing the school and telling them exactly what I think of them for letting you walk out, and asking for a meeting with Mrs Angel and Ali Morgan's parents. And don't you think you aren't in trouble either, Poppy. Now, hand me back to Izzy's dad."

Poppy sighed and passed the phone over. Maybe Mum would calm down…

"Oh, you'll let the school know? OK, good. Yeah, I wouldn't want Mrs Angel thinking I'd kidnapped Poppy. I might not survive," Izzy's dad joked. "I'll bring her back about six-thirty, OK?" He ended the call and sighed. "Your mum sounds like she wants to yell at somebody, Poppy. I wouldn't want to be your school secretary right now. So…" He eyed her thoughtfully. "Exactly what was going on? What did Ali say that made you so upset? Izzy's always telling me how brave you are, and how Ali doesn't worry you at all. She said she wishes *she* could be that cool about it!"

"Dad…" Izzy moaned.

Poppy nodded. "It wasn't actually Ali."

"Who was it then?" Izzy demanded. "Was someone mean to you at lunch or something?"

Poppy stared at her tiredly, and sighed. "Yes. You."

FOUR

Izzy stared at her, her pale-blue eyes going rounder and rounder, and red spots growing in the middle of her cheeks. "I wasn't!" she said, shaking her head in bewilderment.

Poppy sighed. "I don't think you meant to be. Or I don't think so *now*, anyway. But you all went off somewhere without me at lunch, and then this afternoon you kept looking at each other and – and sort of smirking…" She glanced up miserably at Izzy.

Izzy went darkly red all over. "Oh. Yes. I suppose we did. But we weren't trying to be mean at all."

"So what were you doing?" her dad demanded curiously.

Izzy frowned and looked down at her school bag. "Promise you won't be cross?" she asked Poppy.

"It's a bit late for that, Iz!" her dad muttered. "Just tell us."

Izzy reached into her bag and pulled out a crumpled, sticky-looking piece of paper.

"Oh! You got it out of the bin!" Poppy took it, rather sadly. She was wondering now if she ought to have stood up for herself better. Maybe she shouldn't have let Ali convince her that she was a cheat. But there was no way she could enter this now. It had Ribena all over it, she reckoned, and perhaps a bit of chocolate?

"Is that your competition entry, Poppy?" Izzy's dad asked, peering at it interestedly. "It looks very good." He squinted at it sideways. "What's under that splodge there?"

"Scented plants. It was meant to be about all the different senses." Poppy heaved a huge sigh, and nearly caused a tidal wave over the edge of her hot chocolate mug. "I wish I hadn't thrown it away now. I mean, I did borrow ideas, but that isn't really the same as copying, is it?"

"Of course not!" Izzy's dad chuckled. "All designers have to refer back to other famous gardens, Poppy. It's what you do with the ideas that counts. So is this what you were doing at lunch, Iz? It can't have taken you that long to get it out of the bin though."

Izzy shook her head and pulled out another piece

of paper. She slid it across the table to Poppy, looking apologetic. "We thought you were wrong to throw it away, so I got it out of the bin and we were going to just enter it for you. But by then it was all mucked up. So we tried to redo it. It took ages. And it still isn't as good as yours was."

"You did me another copy?" Poppy murmured, looking down at it.

"Well, we tried, but none of us can draw like you, Poppy. It's useless. And we couldn't remember what was in some of the smudgy bits. We were thinking we might have to get together tomorrow again and sort it out." She looked sideways at Poppy. "Are you cross? We just wanted to help."

"I'm not cross. Emily wrote this, didn't she?" Poppy asked, looking at one of the little descriptions. "She's got the worst spelling ever." She shook her head, grinning. The drawings weren't nearly as good as hers, like Izzy said, but they'd obviously tried so hard to make it look like her design. It was the nicest thing they could possibly have done. "So this was why you were looking all weird. I thought you hated me because I was a cheat, like Ali said!"

Izzy stared at her disgustedly. "You thought we'd believe that – that slug! Instead of you? Who do you think we are?"

Poppy shrugged apologetically. "I did stay up a bit late finishing my design," she admitted. "I was so tired... I suppose I was a bit silly – you know. A bit teary. I feel a lot better now though," she added, taking a big gulp of chocolate.

"Good." Izzy's dad was still studying the original design. "Finish up that hot chocolate, you two."

Izzy looked at him in surprise. "Why? We've only just got it."

"Because we need to go home and get Poppy some more paper. We're not wasting this," her dad said firmly. "Brilliant ideas. *Very original*, and I'll tell Ali and her little rat gang that. We're going home so you can do another copy. I'll help. But only from a distance. I won't put a finger near it, so no one can say we were cheating."

"I'm just not sure it's exciting enough..." Poppy murmured thoughtfully. She and Izzy had eaten a super-fast tea of toasted sandwiches before clearing the table and covering it in paper and coloured pencils, and Izzy's dad's huge collection of garden design books. He had flicked through these, carefully pointing out to Poppy where various gardens were described as "inspired by" something.

"Which is just a nice way of saying copied from. Well, no. Not exactly copied. You borrow a bit from their idea and twist it round and make it your own. Which is just what you did, Poppy, I promise."

He even had the same Cam Morris book as Poppy's mum and he snorted disgustedly when Poppy showed it to him, looking at him worriedly to see if he thought she'd "borrowed" too much.

"It's nothing like yours!" he told her indignantly. "Do you know, I'm worried that Ali's going to end up running the country one day. She seems to be able to twist all of you round her little finger."

"You know you wanted it to be more exciting?" Izzy said thoughtfully, leaning over Poppy's shoulder.

Poppy looked up at her hopefully.

"In that video, Cam Morris talked about everybody being able to help in the garden, and get involved, and do stuff. I mean, there's lots to look at, and smell, and touch, and it's beautiful, but do you think it would help if there were things we could *do*?"

Poppy nodded, frowning. "It would. What, though? I can't think of anything…"

"What about a weather station?" Izzy asked hopefully. She was really into science, and loved experiments. She had the biggest chemistry set Poppy had ever seen. "We could even build the instruments ourselves – I know a website. There's a cool wind vane you can make out of old DVDs…"

"None of my DVDs count as old," her dad said quickly. "And actually, I've got another idea. I know you've got herbs in the garden for the Taste section, Poppy, but what about vegetables too? And fruit! You've got a lovely south-facing wall here, look. You could even have a peach tree growing up there!"

"Do you think school would use the vegetables in our school lunches?" Poppy asked, her eyes widening hopefully.

Izzy frowned. "We'd have to have ever such a lot for that. But if we grew salad, I bet that would be useful."

"It's worth trying anyway," her dad mused. "Growing your own's a really interesting idea. Lots of schools are putting in gardens now. Since Jamie Oliver made all those TV programmes about how bad school meals were, schools are trying really hard with their lunches. Some nice fresh salad would be great. And I'm sure they could use your herbs too, Poppy. And you could try to grow everything organically."

Poppy nodded slowly. "I was thinking about that. It sounds good, not having any chemicals, but what if bugs just eat everything we plant? Mum tried to grow broad beans last year, and in the end she just pulled them up. They had these disgusting little black flies all over them. All over! They were covered."

Izzy's dad sighed. "Tell me about it. It's so difficult. I've started suggesting to people that they put ponds in their gardens if they want to grow fruit and veg and not spray them with anything."

Poppy wrinkled her nose and Izzy stared at her dad. "What good does a pond do?" she demanded.

Poppy smiled down at her garden design. She was glad Izzy didn't know either. She hadn't felt like asking in case it made her sound stupid.

"Frogs." Izzy's dad folded his arms and grinned at them. "Think about it."

"Oh!" Poppy looked up. "They eat the flies? Really? Does it make a difference?"

"Well, it helps a bit. It's still a problem though. You have to be really watchful and sneaky. Planting marigolds round your tomatoes, that sort of thing. Pests don't like marigolds. Or basil! You can plant basil next to your tomatoes to keep flies off, and then you've got tomato and basil soup." He beamed at them, obviously thinking he was being very funny.

Izzy rolled her eyes at him, but Poppy chewed her pencil thoughtfully and frowned down at her design. "It's an awful lot to remember. I don't think we have to work out the exact plants we want to use now though. It's more like the shape of the garden. We could put vegetables here..." she murmured, pointing at the Taste section. "Peach tree up against this wall... Maybe even a little greenhouse in the corner here!" she added hopefully. "And the weather station bits wouldn't need a whole lot of space, would they?" she asked Izzy.

"Oh, no. You could put that wind vane on a pole anywhere," Izzy agreed. "And a rain gauge wouldn't take much space either. You could explain that you're having them so that people in the school can take measurements every day. And they'd help with growing food – we'd know how much rain there'd been, and so whether we needed to water the plants."

"Yes, but wouldn't we just know if it had been raining?" Poppy asked, and Izzy's dad snorted with laughter.

"She's got a point, Iz."

"It isn't the same as being scientific about it," Izzy said firmly.

"I can't look…" Poppy muttered, staring down at the table. "Are loads of people giving their designs in?"

"Nope." Izzy shook her head. "Hardly any. I've got mine, and there's Nick, and Lara; we knew about them already. And Ali, of course. Looks like Lucy and Elspeth didn't dare do their own. Molly, Tilda – oh, and Jake. I wouldn't have thought he'd enter. But that's all. So, eight from our class. Maybe fifty or sixty from the whole school?"

Poppy blinked. Izzy was unfairly quick at working things like that out.

Emily leaned over. "No, all of Year Three had to enter – Mrs Taggart made them. Toby was throwing a wobbly about it. But you needn't worry, Poppy. Toby's design was a line of toilets, with flowers in."

That made Poppy look up. "Why?"

"Oh, there's a house round the corner from us in the village with a toilet full of flowers. James and Toby think it's the funniest thing ever, so he thought school would like a loo garden too. Honestly, Poppy, yours deserves to win."

Poppy smiled at her. "If it does, Izzy and her dad have won too. They gave me loads of ideas."

"Don't start stressing about whether you copied it again!" Izzy told her sternly. "We'll all scream."

"I promise," Poppy said meekly. "And if Ali says anything I'll just pretend I can't hear her."

It was a good thing that Poppy had decided just to ignore Ali, because two weeks later Mrs Angel announced in assembly that Poppy's design had been chosen as the school entry. Mrs Brooker in the office had had Poppy's design blown up to poster size, and there was a big display all about the competition in the main corridor on the way in, where all the parents could see it.

Ali was spitting.

"I reckon Mrs Brooker needs a security camera on that poster," Emily said thoughtfully, the morning after the announcement. The whole class had gone through the main corridor on the way to IT, and Ali had glared at the poster hatefully.

"She did look as though she fancied shredding it to bits with her nails," Maya agreed. "If anything does happen to it, we so know who it was."

Poppy shivered. "She keeps giving me the meanest looks. I'm really glad the design's all sent off now. I mean, there's nothing she can do about it."

Izzy nodded slowly. "Ye-e-es… But just remember how horrible she was before – how much she got to you."

"Izzy! Don't be such a gloom!" Emily snapped.

Izzy shrugged. "I'm not trying to be. I just think Poppy needs to be careful," she argued, wriggling round to look at Emily. They were all sitting squashed up together on one of the playground benches at lunchtime. It was the middle of April now, and the weather was finally getting a bit warmer. It was warm enough to sit still, anyway.

"Oh no…" Poppy muttered. "Look, it's like we called her over or something. We shouldn't talk about her, ever!"

Ali was stalking towards them, flanked by Lucy and Elspeth, as always.

"Did your mum ever do anything about making Mrs Angel have a meeting with her parents?" Izzy whispered.

"No, I talked her out of it," Poppy whispered back, out of the side of her mouth. "I said I was really tired and I'd just taken what Ali said the wrong way. She knew how late I was up that night, so she gave in. I had to stop her – Mrs Angel's like a demon for people twisting the truth. She'd have worked it all out, and then it would have been awful."

"I suppose you think you're really clever?" Ali snarled as soon as she got close to them. She'd obviously been working up to this ever since she found out she hadn't won. She was white in the face, and her eyes were slitted with fury.

"She is, actually," Maya said, smiling sweetly at Ali. "A lot cleverer than you, anyway."

"Everyone knows you cheated," Ali snapped, ignoring Maya. Since she'd found out that Maya's mum was famous, she always tried to keep on her good side, so she just pretended she hadn't heard.

Poppy flinched a little, but she just stared back at Ali. "I didn't," she said flatly.

Ali seemed rather surprised. Perhaps she'd been expecting Poppy to protest, or maybe cry. Such a matter-of-fact denial wasn't what she wanted at all.

"You did," she said half-heartedly.

Poppy and the others just stared at her. Poppy could feel Izzy on one side of her and Maya on the other. Izzy was so furious she was actually trembling, practically vibrating with crossness. Poppy could almost feel her saying, *Ignore her! Ignore her! She's just horrible.* And it helped. She simply stared blankly back at Ali and didn't say anything.

Ali glared at them all, going whiter than ever, so that little red patches showed up on her cheekbones. Poppy knew from arguing with Alex and Jake that there was nothing more annoying than people refusing to join in an argument when you really wanted to yell at them. For a moment she almost felt sorry for Ali, who'd clearly worked herself up to have a massive, blazing row. But only almost.

"Don't sit there looking so smug," Ali snarled. "You cheated, and I should have won. I definitely should." Then the fury melted out of her face – it was quite horrible to watch, as though she was wax, and the frown lines just melted away. They were replaced with a very sweet, very nasty smile. "You'll wish I had. You really will, Poppy." She giggled. "We'll get you back in your own way too."

FIVE

Poppy had tried her best not to worry about what Ali had said, but it was tricky. She'd looked so spooky, with her white face and her eyes all glittery like that. And what had she meant about getting Poppy back in her own way? It was eerie. Even Emily, who was usually unfazed by Ali's nastiness, said it had sent shivers down her spine.

Poppy couldn't help glancing round at Ali and Lucy and Elspeth every so often for the rest of the day. But they just smirked at her, and it left her feeling edgier than ever. She was glad that it was a Thursday, and there was only one more day of school before the weekend. Perhaps Ali would forget about it?

"She's not giving you funny looks any more." Izzy muttered before school the next morning. "Actually…"

"What?" Poppy asked anxiously, trying to look

at Ali without being obvious. Izzy sounded oddly surprised.

"She looks quite pleased about something. Maybe she's given up being annoyed about the garden thing!"

"I hope so," Poppy agreed, feeling a lot better. "After all, just because I won our school's competition, it doesn't mean anything! Thousands of schools are going to enter!" The strange sinking feeling in her stomach eased away and Poppy suddenly wished she'd eaten more breakfast. She was starving now. Luckily Mum had made her a huge packed lunch as usual, so she got her lunchbox out and grabbed an apple, biting into it quickly before the bell went.

Still, the apple didn't make up for her usual toast, even when she always had to fight it out of the hands of Jake and Alex, who could easily eat a whole loaf between them at breakfast. Poppy practically dragged Izzy and the others into the lunch room, and dived gratefully into their class box to grab her lunch. "I'm so hungry…" she moaned, pulling out her sandwiches.

"Yeah, we saw you chewing on your pencil all the way through IT," Emily agreed. "I thought you were

60

going to eat the whole thing."

"It's all in my teeth," Poppy admitted, shuddering.

Maya sniggered. "Maybe you'll come up with an amazing new remedy. Lead – it must be really good for something."

"Actually, lead's poisonous," Izzy pointed out. "But it's OK, Poppy," she added quickly, seeing Poppy go white. "They don't actually put lead in pencils. They never did. The grey bit's made of graphite."

Poppy didn't say anything. She just kept staring into her lunchbox, her cheese and dandelion sandwich halfway to her mouth.

"Honestly." Izzy gazed at her worriedly. "I didn't mean to upset you. There really isn't anything poisonous in pencils, I promise."

"You didn't upset me," Poppy whispered. She pushed her lunchbox across the table towards Izzy and Maya, who were sitting opposite. "Look."

"Your lunch can't be that bad," Emily said, leaning over to see. "And if you will get your mum to make you those stupid sandwiches, you can't really complain. Did you get a slug in one?" Then she frowned, her nose wrinkling. "What's *that*?"

"I don't know," Poppy whispered, watching wide-eyed as Izzy lifted out the little clay figure. It looked like it was made of that special modelling clay you could bake in the oven. It came in lots of bright colours. She'd got some somewhere…

"Did – did your mum put that in?" Maya asked, looking confused.

"No!" Poppy said, in horror. "Of course she didn't! Why would she?" She swallowed, gulping in a breath. "And it wasn't there this morning when I got my apple out," she added.

The four of them stared at the little figure lying on the table. It looked a tiny bit like Poppy – as much a clay figure that was only about five centimetres high could. It had longish, yellowish-brown hair, with a few blue and green streaks. It could almost have been cute, except that the mouth was much too big for the face, and it was wide open, with nasty little teeth modelled out of white bits of clay all round the edges. It was either shouting at somebody, or crying. It was horrible.

"Someone *made* that of me," Poppy whispered. "It's one of those things you stick pins in. I can't believe someone did that…"

"Someone!" Maya exploded. "We know exactly who!" She nodded across the room at Ali's table. She and Lucy and Elspeth had chosen to sit very close, funnily enough. They were staring at Poppy over their sandwiches, smirking. Until Miss Grace walked past on lunch duty, and they suddenly looked all angelic.

Izzy nodded. "We can't prove it though. And they'd never admit it. Are you OK, Poppy? Do you want to go and tell someone?"

Poppy shook her head. "What good would that do? You're right, we can't prove it was Ali."

Emily was frowning. "Are we sure it *was* her though?"

"Who else would do something like that to Poppy?" Izzy asked her.

"Mmm. I know. But Ali's never been into – you know. Spells and witchy stuff. Has she? When Maisie had that stupid book all about spells last year, Ali told her she was totally thick and it was all rubbish. So why would she start doing that stuff now?"

Maya shrugged. "Since when has she ever behaved like a normal person?"

Poppy zipped her lunchbox shut and put it on the floor by her feet, leaving the figure lying in the centre of the table, until Izzy put a piece of kitchen foil over it and scrunched it up in her hand. Even though it was just modelling clay, no one wanted to touch it.

"Shall I throw it away?" Izzy asked, and Poppy

nodded, watching her as she threaded her way across the dining hall to the bins.

"Aren't you going to eat your lunch?" Izzy asked when she got back.

"I'm not really hungry any more," Poppy said, her voice very small.

"You were starving," Maya reminded her gently. "Do you want one of my sandwiches?"

Poppy looked at her gratefully. "I know it's stupid. It just feels like everything in my lunch is sort of…"

"Spoiled," Izzy agreed, nodding. "Look. Chocolate fingers." She passed half her packet over to Poppy, and Emily gave her some cheese cubes.

"I still don't understand why she's doing it," Emily muttered. "It works though, doesn't it? I wouldn't eat your lunch either. Maybe tomorrow you'd better keep it in your rucksack."

"Ali could still get at it," Poppy murmured. "If she tried hard enough."

"I shouldn't think she'd do the same thing again," Izzy said thoughtfully. "She's too clever." She shrugged as they all stared at her. "She actually is. She may be mean, but you've got to admit, she's very, very good at being horrible. Isn't she?"

Poppy giggled. "I suppose she is." She sighed. "Ali's

going to do something else then, you reckon?"

Izzy gave her an apologetic look. "Um, probably. But it's all stupid. It doesn't mean anything."

"Even if there was such a thing as magic, Ali definitely can't do it," Maya said firmly.

"And there isn't," Emily said, elbowing her.

"Of course there isn't!" Maya added quickly.

"I know," Poppy agreed, but she didn't feel as sure as she wished she did.

They finished their lunches quickly – no one felt very hungry any more, somehow – and headed out to the playground, where they huddled up thoughtfully on the grassy bank in the sun.

"I keep looking round for Ali," Poppy muttered, peering across the playground.

"Mmmm, I know…" Izzy ageed. Then she grinned and nudged Poppy with her elbow. "Just try and think of her as a witch like the one in *The Wizard of Oz*. All green and with a really huge pointy nose."

Maya nodded. "Or isn't there a story about a witch who had chicken's feet? Ali would look great with little scaly chicken legs."

They kept swapping stories about uglier, nastier witches until the bell went, and Poppy was starting to feel quite cheered up. It helped that Ali hadn't come anywhere near them since they left the dining hall. They hadn't even seen her.

But then as they got up to go back into school, she suddenly popped up out of nowhere – and Poppy was so jumpy that it almost seemed like magic. She was suddenly there, looking worryingly happy. She smiled sweetly at Poppy and said, "Just stand still!"

Poppy was too surprised to do anything else. She froze, and then wondered if Ali was going to throw something at her. She wanted to run, but somehow she couldn't work out which way to go.

Lucy and Elspeth dived out from behind Ali with something in their hands, and Poppy flinched, expecting that they really were going to throw it, whatever it was.

But they crouched down on the ground behind her and started drawing on the asphalt. It was chalk that they were holding, sticks of red chalk.

Poppy gaped at them, and Izzy grabbed her arm and pulled at her. "Come on, Poppy. It's just another stupid joke."

"What are they doing?" Poppy muttered. "I don't understand." Her heart was thudding and bouncing, and she wished she hadn't eaten any of the others'

lunches after all. She felt sick.

"There!" Elspeth and Lucy stood up triumphantly, leaving a vague red figure outlined on the playground.

"Your shadow…" Maya said uneasily, and the four of them drew back, watching, as Ali walked round to the far side of the figure and stood still for a moment, with her eyes closed and her lips moving. They couldn't tell what she was saying, which just made it all the more weird. Then she opened her eyes, smiled at Poppy and started to rub the figure out with the toe of her shoe, very slowly, very deliberately, watching Poppy the whole time. A small, interested audience had gathered, mostly girls from their class, pointing, and whispering.

"That's *horrible*," Maya spat out disgustedly. "Poppy, come on." She grabbed Poppy's other arm, and she and Izzy hauled her back towards the classroom.

"That was another spell then," Poppy whispered as they sat down. "What do you think it was supposed to do?"

"Nothing!" Izzy snapped. "Don't even think about it."

"It was like she was rubbing *me* out," Poppy said.

Izzy kicked her under the table, but not very hard.

"Smile. Now. Look as though you don't care. They're coming."

Ali and Lucy and Elspeth hurried in, huddled in a giggling group and followed by the other girls from the class who'd been watching. *Everyone* stared at Poppy.

Poppy folded her arms and smiled as convincingly as she could. She had a feeling she looked really strange, but at least she was there, and she wasn't falling over, or fainting, or whatever a rubbed-out person was supposed to do. *It doesn't mean anything*, she told herself. *It's stupid. It's all rubbish.*

She noticed that Ali looked slightly disappointed, which was good. She felt pleased about that, but only in a vague, distant sort of way. Most of her was just desperate to go home and spend the weekend hiding under her duvet.

"Guess who I saw on Saturday!" Maya came racing up to Poppy and Izzy on Monday morning, with Emily hurrying behind her.

Poppy shrugged, and then felt a bit guilty and tried to look interested. She'd spent the whole weekend trying to forget about Ali's stupid spells, and then suddenly remembering them and feeling awful all over again. On Friday night she'd even dreamed about that strange shadow figure. Ali had rubbed it out, but it had been the real Poppy who disappeared instead. Then the chalk figure had got up and walked into the classroom and sat down in Poppy's place, and no one had noticed.

She'd woken up crying, and her dad had come up to see what was wrong. He'd hugged her and made her a cup of hot chocolate. She'd been so upset he'd let her go downstairs with him to make it, even though it was about midnight. Then he'd sat on the end of her bed for ages, while she tried to get back to sleep.

"Who?" Poppy asked.

"The Wicked Witch of the West," Maya murmured, leaning close. "And the other two. I can't think of any more witch names... Anyway. They were in the bookshop."

"Exciting!" Emily twitched her eyebrows up and down, and Poppy actually laughed. It felt better being back with her friends, people who knew what was going on. She'd almost told Dad on Friday night, but she'd been so tired and jumpy and just plain scared that she hadn't wanted to talk about it.

"Shut up!" Maya sighed. "I went in with my dad,

and they were there. You know Elspeth's weird laugh?"

The others nodded. Elspeth sounded as though she had the hiccups when she was laughing; it was unmistakable.

"I heard her, so I went to see what they were doing. They were in the bit with all the health books – the section on healing and all the stuff that you like, Poppy. And guess what's next to all the books about remedies?"

"Gardening?" Poppy asked vaguely, trying to remember. Most of her books had come from the shop that sold the essential oils, not the bookshop.

"Nope. Occult." Maya looked at them all impatiently. "That means witchy stuff. And they were looking at books from both, Poppy. They're right next to each other. That's why they're doing it! They think you're into spells too. She said she was going to get you back in your own way, didn't she?"

"But I don't do any of that stuff!" Poppy said indignantly.

"Yes, *we* know that. But Ali just thinks it's all the same, I bet. She thinks you're really into spells and potions. Eye of newt, fingernails of bat. All of that stuff. And don't tell me bats don't have fingernails, Iz, because I know!"

Izzy closed her mouth with a snap and gave Maya an apologetic grin.

Emily suddenly laughed – an excited, conspiratorial sort of laugh.

Maya nodded. "I know! It's perfect!"

"What is?" Poppy demanded, frowning.

"They must think you know loads about witchcraft, Poppy," Emily said eagerly. "Everyone at school knows you're always coming up with weird stuff, like putting cobwebs on cuts."

"That works," Poppy said stubbornly.

"Maybe. But it sounds really witchy, doesn't it?" Emily stared at her, and Poppy sighed.

"I suppose it does a bit," she admitted.

"And," Maya put in, "I bet they've scared themselves reading all those – umm, what's it called again? Oh, *occult*. Occult books. Lucy looked really spooked in the bookshop. They were reading out a spell about bringing dead things back to life, and she kept trying to tell Ali to stop it, as though she thought it was going to happen in the middle of the Gardening section."

"I still don't see what you were laughing about," Poppy murmured with a little shiver. She felt the tiniest bit sorry for Lucy.

"Well, don't you think we could pretend?" Maya asked. "If they already think you're a witch, why don't you just be one?"

Emily nodded eagerly. "They'll definitely believe in spells you put on them. We could scare them silly. I bet we could."

"I could find you some spells," Izzy suggested. "I bet there's loads of stuff we could find on the Net."

Poppy looked round at the three of them, all so excited, and wondered why she didn't feel excited too. It was a good plan, she could see that. But somehow she didn't like it. And even though she didn't believe in Ali's spells, the thought of trying some of her own made her feel shivery.

"Are you OK?" Izzy asked, sounding rather worried.

"Oh!" Poppy gave a little jump and nearly spilled her orange juice all over the floor. "Sorry, I was just thinking…"

"You haven't said a word for ages," Izzy explained. "And you look miserable."

"Sorry…" Poppy repeated, sighing. Izzy probably wished she hadn't come round. Poppy wasn't exactly great company.

"You're still really worried about Ali and that shadow spell, aren't you?" Izzy said thoughtfully. "Or is it the clay doll? I thought it was the shadow one that got to you most. I think it would have got to me as well."

Poppy shook her head. "I don't think it would! Why is it only me that's really fussing about it? They put that stuff on your coat too."

Izzy sniffed. This afternoon, when they'd gone to get their things at home time, she and Poppy had both found weird marks all over their coats. Emily had looked at them and said it was definitely snail slime.

"Or maybe slug…" she'd added, eyeing it with her head on one side and a frowning look, as though she ought to be able to tell the difference. "Oh, come on, don't look at me like that! Toby and James have snails *everywhere*. There was a snail crawling along the side of our bath this morning."

Emily always made Poppy feel really grateful that she had older brothers instead of younger ones.

The tacky, silvery slime was in weird swirly patterns that looked like they ought to mean something. It was sickening.

"How do you think they got the snails to do that?"

she asked Izzy now, taking a gulp of juice to cover up how much she hated talking about it.

Izzy shrugged. "Waved a lettuce leaf in front of them, I suppose. But you know Ali. She could even make a snail do what she wanted. It would have taken ages though. They must have sneaked into the cloakroom at lunchtime and done it then. If only we'd known, we could have set Miss Grace on them." She sighed.

Poppy set down her glass and gaped at her. "You really aren't bothered at all!" she said, almost shouting. "Why aren't you?"

Izzy stared back at her. "Poppy, it's only Ali doing her normal horrible stuff. It's just – a bit dressed up, that's all." She shuffled closer and put an arm round her friend's shoulders. "Sorry, Poppy, I didn't see how much it was getting to you. OK. We really have to get her to stop." Izzy glared at her determinedly. "I know you hate the spells idea but I think it's the only thing that's going to work."

"I know I'm a wuss," Poppy admitted. "But it's scary. When you said you'd look up spells… please don't, Izzy. I don't want to use real spells – ones that people who actually want to be witches use."

Izzy shrugged. "No problem. We'll make up our

74

own. Oh, come on, Poppy, it'll be easy. We've only got to make them good enough to convince Ali, after all."

SIX

"A day off school? Everyone's going to want to go!" Emily pointed out as they read the letters Mr Finlay was passing round at the end of school the next day.

"There's only thirty places. But I want to," Maya agreed. "It sounds really good. I've never been to Amberlake."

"Ohhh, it's nice! It's a massive stately home," Emily said enthusiastically. "The house is quite cool. I mean, you can look at the kitchens, and dress up in old-fashioned clothes, that sort of thing. But the gardens are brilliant. They go down to the lake, and there's a stream, and huge trees. And even though it's all really beautiful, none of it says don't walk on the grass or anything like that. They do great Easter-egg hunts."

"Do you think we'll get to see everything?" Maya asked, sounding hopeful. "The announcement about

76

the winning school's at two o'clock – and we're going in the morning, it says. Take a packed lunch… Oh, that's loads of time." She beamed at Poppy. "Let's support our brilliant entry by Poppy Martin, it says. You're Mrs Angel's favourite person now, definitely. If you win, you'll probably get a free pass off SATs or something."

Poppy went pink. "It's exciting," she admitted. "I wish I knew how many schools had entered. This is only the announcement for schools close to us. I suppose it means someone from round here must have won…" She made a face at the letter. "This is going to start Ali off again, isn't it?"

Izzy eyed her. "Probably. So we need to get on with our spells too."

Poppy nodded reluctantly. "I know. It just isn't me – that's all. I don't think I'll be able to make them believe it. I can't see me chanting anything…"

"I bet you could make a better doll than Ali did," Emily suggested.

"Ugh. No." Poppy shook her head. "I'm definitely not doing that."

Emily rolled her eyes, and sighed. "You're not making this easy, you know."

"I know… Oh!" Poppy suddenly brightened up.

"What about a ghost? I almost believe in ghosts. Sometimes when it's dark, anyway."

"A ghost…" Maya said thoughtfully. "A ghost that's out to get Ali? I like it!"

Izzy frowned. "But there isn't a ghost at school. There'd be loads of stories about it if there was. Ali isn't going to believe us if we just invent a new ghost, is she?"

"She might," Emily said stubbornly. "We could say that one of the mirrors in the girls' toilets is haunted. We could write messages on it in lipstick."

"A haunted toilet?" Poppy sniggered a little, and then started to laugh properly. It felt as though she'd had something tied tight round her middle, and it was loosening at last.

Emily glared for a second and then started laughing as well. "OK. Maybe not then."

"But I still like the ghost idea," Poppy said thoughtfully. "There must be some way to use it – maybe we could pretend Ali's house has a ghost. No, I know! Amberlake! A big old house like that could have loads of ghosts! We can haunt Ali at the announcement ceremony!"

"Do you think she'll go though?" Izzy asked. "What if she's sulking?"

Poppy sighed. "Of course she'll go. There might be some way for her to get me into trouble, or show me up or something. She's not going to miss that, is she?"

Emily glanced over her shoulder as they went out to the cloakroom. "They're definitely all staring at the letter," she reported. "Ali looks pretty determined. I think you're right, Poppy."

Poppy nodded. "OK then. I don't mind pretending to summon a ghost." She shrugged her jacket on and wrapped it round her tightly. "We can make one up. But nothing too gory!"

Poppy's mum wasn't working that day, so she got to go straight home instead of going to after-school club. She stretched out on her bed with Mum's laptop propped up in front of her – she'd told Mum she needed to look up some stuff about an author for homework, which was actually true. But Poppy had got all the answers she needed in about five minutes, which meant that now she was looking at the Amberlake website and trying to work out what sort of ghost there should be.

She clicked on Explore the House, and watched a slideshow about the different rooms, but it wasn't very exciting – or it would have been, if she'd just wanted to go and visit, but it was no good for ghost stories. She sighed gustily. It would be nice just to go and see it all, without worrying about ghosts. There was a whole room made out of seashells, and a Chinese Bedroom with amazing red walls. And the paintings – whole rooms covered in paintings. From the slideshow it did look like quite a lot of them were those weird paintings of piles of dead birds, but she liked looking at the portraits when they went to old houses. Mum loved visiting them when they went on holiday, and Poppy usually went with her. They always made things up about the people in the portraits. It was fun.

Portraits… Poppy's eyes widened and she clicked back to the section on the history of the house. If she could find a portrait, and a name, couldn't they make up a ghost story about someone who'd really lived at Amberlake? That would make it sound a lot more real.

The family who'd built the house in the 1700s were called Bayley, Poppy discovered, skimming the page. None of them looked very exciting in their portraits though – they all seemed to have very long thin noses… Or maybe that was just how it was fashionable to look back then?

The house had been sold to a Lord Morrell after that. Poppy sighed. None of this was very thrilling, either. Lord Morrell had died in bed aged eighty-two. Typical.

Ooh, but this was better. His daughter, Sophia, had died very young – and there was a portrait of her! Poppy clicked on it eagerly. It was a lovely picture anyway, but for a person who needed to invent a ghost story, it was perfect. Sophia Morrell stared mournfully out of the portrait, with a little white dog clutched in her arms. She had a green dress on, silk or satin or something shiny – the fabric seemed to glow out from the painting. Her eyes were huge and dark – it was the eyes that made her look so sad, Poppy decided, as well as the little droop at the corner of her mouth. She wondered if Sophia's father had been happy with the portrait. Would anybody really want to see their child looking so sad every time they walked past a painting? Maybe her parents had refused to pay the painter.

Poppy nibbled her bottom lip thoughtfully. She liked making up stories. She wasn't as good at literacy as Maya, because somehow her stories didn't always work when she wrote them down, but she loved the ideas for stories. Sophia's parents had wanted her portrait painted because she was so beautiful, and surely she was going to be married soon – Poppy looked back at the dates on the website. The portrait had been painted in 1793, when Sophia was fifteen. Back then people did get married very young – the girls anyway. She sniggered to herself. Jake and Alex were fifteen. She couldn't imagine either of them getting married.

But Sophia Morrell might have been just at the right age to fall in love with somebody (there were a whole lot of fifteen-year-old girls who were mad enough to fancy Jake and Alex, after all). And she was bound to fall in love with the wrong person, Poppy thought to herself, grabbing her pad and starting to draw Sophia – the big eyes, pale face, shining honey-coloured hair. If you were fifteen and you spent days and days wearing your best dress and staring at a handsome young painter (Poppy had no idea if Francis Rowley was handsome or young, but for the purposes of her story he was eighteen and gorgeous) surely you'd fall in love with him. Poppy drew him – with some paintbrushes and floppy hair. And then your father – Lord Morrell was a bit boring in his official portrait, so Poppy decided to make his moustache bigger in her version – said you couldn't ever marry a penniless portrait painter, and besides, he'd already arranged for you to marry the boring oldest son of the Lord next door.

Anyone with any sense of drama – and it was obvious from her portrait that Sophia was very dramatic – would go out and walk up and down the lake in the dark feeling totally miserable, and then accidentally fall in and drown. The portrait painter would turn up just too late to rescue her – but in time for Sophia to tell him that she would love him for always, and she was going to haunt Amberlake to make her mean father's descendants as miserable as she was.

Poppy happily scribbled away, drawing Sophia dying in her painter's arms, and then her ghost, still in the green dress, walking over the surface of the lake.

"We can call her the Green Lady," Poppy muttered happily to herself. She put the laptop down on the floor next to her bed and then rolled over and stared up at the ceiling. Now she just had to work out a way to use her ghost to scare Ali.

It had been such a strange few days, eerie and horrible, and she was still dreaming about the shadow, and waking up in the middle of the night.

Poppy yawned. Her bed was so comfortable, and the room was warm.

A thin green figure danced across the water, darting in and out of the sunny patches and the reeds around the lake, her green dress merging into the tall stems. She fluttered and blinked in and out as the light caught her, and Poppy strained her eyes to see.

The figure came gradually closer, stretching her hands to Poppy. It was hard to see her face – she was like a flickery reflection on the water instead of a proper solid person, but Poppy was sure that she was smiling. Poppy was quite certain that she was a ghost – her Green Lady, but she wasn't frightened. Sophia wanted to help…

Poppy blinked and yawned, and stared at the ceiling in puzzlement, still seeing faint greenish patterns behind her eyes. She'd been dreaming…

Then she remembered what she'd been dreaming about, and sat up with a start. She'd imagined herself an awfully real-looking ghost. But even though she'd hated the thought of pretending to be a witch, she was actually looking forward to this now. She'd made Sophia's story up, so it was silly to feel that Sophia approved of what they were going to do, but Poppy couldn't help it. That flittery greenish figure had been laughing. She wanted Poppy to get back at Ali, just as she'd wanted to get back at her bullying father in Poppy's story.

And Poppy's dream had told her exactly how to do it too – the first part of it anyway. She just needed to get herself and Iz and Maya and Emily somewhere Ali could hear them, and tell them all about her dream.

"Well, it tasted horrible," Poppy said, glaring at Emily, who was smirking at her and trying to make her giggle. "But you have to put up with that kind of thing. They're very powerful herbs, and they make it absolutely certain you'll have true dreams. Is she listening?" she added to Izzy in the breath of a whisper.

"Oh, definitely," Izzy whispered back, looking cautiously sideways round the seat of the coach. "They all are. So what did you see?" she asked more loudly.

"A figure…" Poppy hissed dramatically. "Dressed in green, floating across a stretch of water – but it was strange; the water was an odd colour, almost golden." She paused, and then stretched her foot under the seat in front to kick Emily, who'd missed her cue.

"Oh!" Emily nodded. "Golden? That sounds like Amberlake, Poppy. It's the stones around the edge of the lake – they're a sort of yellowy colour, and it makes the water look amber. The house is named after it. Wow, isn't it weird that you dreamed about Amberlake, when we're going there!"

Poppy shook her head. "Not really. I told you, that spell always gives you true dreams. Special ones. Almost more like a foretelling than a dream."

"Maybe you saw the Amberlake ghost!" Maya said excitedly, remembering her lines a bit better than Emily. They'd worked it all out, but it was harder to say the story naturally when they knew Ali and the other two were listening.

"Is there one?" Izzy asked.

"Oh yes!" Maya nodded. "I looked it up; we've got a National Trust guidebook. The ghost's really famous – she's called the Green Lady. She's a girl who fell in love with someone she wasn't allowed to marry, and then she died in a horrible accident by the lake. And now she haunts Amberlake, seeking revenge."

Poppy shuddered. She'd come up with this story but it sounded ever so real. "Revenge on who?" she asked, her voice rather squeaky. At least it would make it sound real to Ali too.

Maya shook her head thoughtfully. "I'm not sure – I suppose her family, but they died hundreds of years ago now. You called her up, Poppy. Don't you know?"

Poppy swallowed. This was the important bit. "Not really. I know in the dream she wanted to help me – she stretched out her hands and smiled, and I was sure she was friendly. But I didn't know about the revenge thing…" She paused, for just long enough, and then added, "I wonder what she'll do?"

"Oh look, look!" Emily whispered, peeping through the gap between the seats. "Ali's gone white, and Lucy and Elspeth are arguing. Elspeth looks like she can see a ghost right now, walking down the bus to get her. Oh!" She whisked herself round as Lucy got up and called down the aisle.

"Mr Finlay! Elspeth thinks she's going to be sick!"

"Awww, poor Elspeth!" Emily giggled.

"Don't forget the bag," Izzy reminded Poppy.

"It's OK, I've got it. I'm still not sure it's going to work though." Poppy slung the bag over her shoulder. It had her lunch in it, but also a bundle of green silky fabric – a huge scarf that belonged to

Maya's mum. Poppy had been a bit worried about borrowing it, but Maya said her mum had so many clothes she probably wouldn't even notice it had gone.

"It will work," Maya said definitely. "You didn't see Ali's face. I was watching, and she absolutely believed you. I told you they scared themselves with all those books. She's been so awful to you, and now the Green Lady's going to get her back."

Mr Finlay had explained to everyone on the trip that there would be a guided tour of the house first, and then a chance to explore in small groups. They had to meet back at the picnic area for lunch, and then Cam Morris himself was going to be there for the announcement at two o'clock.

Usually, Poppy would have really enjoyed the house tour, but she was too bound up in their ghost story to pay much attention. At least their plan to get Ali back was stopping her being nervous about the announcement later on. The one thing she did really want to see was Sophia's portrait – she was sure it would look very different full-size instead of as a little photo on Mum's laptop.

"Oh, look," she whispered as they walked into one of the smaller drawing rooms, its walls papered in a green, leafy pattern. "That's her!" She walked forward, hardly noticing the others around her. She'd almost expected to be disappointed, after thinking so much about Sophia and turning her into a ghost. Let alone that strange dream. But seeing the painting, she felt as though she knew Sophia, almost as well as she knew her best friends.

"Wow, she looks like you," Izzy whispered.

"Does she?" Poppy asked, surprised.

"Mmm. Izzy's right," Emily agreed. "Just give her some blue and green streaks and put her in a floaty sort of skirt and she'd look *exactly* like you."

Poppy went a little closer and lifted her hand, wishing she could stroke the surface of the painting – she was almost sure she'd be able to feel the stiff silk of Sophia's dress or the warmth of her hand. But the guide was watching and she didn't dare.

Oddly enough, now that she saw the real painting, Sophia was smiling. Just a little. Her face was sad, but if you caught the portrait in the right light, there was a funny little quirk at the corner of her mouth.

Poppy smiled back. It was going to work. Everything was going to be all right. Everything.

"We should do it here," she whispered to the others, glancing round and seeing Ali staring worriedly at the painting. Poppy smiled at her, a tiny smile like Sophia's, and Ali's eyes widened.

"Not wait until we're by the lake?" Izzy asked.

"No. She isn't going to go down to the lake, not if she's got any sense, not after the story we told. Is she?"

Emily scowled. "We should have thought of that."

Poppy shook her head. "It doesn't matter. It'll be easier inside anyway. Once we split up, I bet they'll stay in the house."

Poppy was right. Most of the group spilled outside as soon as the tour was over, desperate to go running across the lawns and explore the lakeside. Mr Finlay had given them all dire warnings about staying in groups and being back at the right time, but as they were the older ones they could explore without the teachers. Ali and Lucy and Elspeth gathered in a little huddle by the main hallway, obviously trying to work out where to go, and Poppy and the others sat outside, watching through the big windows, trying to work out when it was safe to dart back in and follow them.

"Oh, they're going back up the stairs!" Maya jumped up and they all hurried back into the hallway. "I think they're going back to that little room with the painting! Ali saw you staring at it. She probably wants to look at it again and see if she can find out who it is."

Poppy nodded. Then she caught her breath excitedly, her eyes sparkling. "We can go the other way up the staircase and get there first. I bet we can. They think that painting's the Green Lady, so let's prove it!" She raced up the stairs, which divided halfway up to lead to the different sides of the house. The little green room was almost in the middle, its windows looking out on to the lake at the back of the house.

They hurried through the rooms, slowing down to a polite walk every time they saw other visitors – the house was very busy with school groups, all there for the competition later on.

"They aren't here yet," Poppy said with a gasp of relief as they darted into Sophia's room. She yanked the gauzy scarf out of her bag, shaking it out so the folds shimmered and floated in the dusty air.

Izzy shivered. "If I were Ali, I'd think that was a ghost," she said. "And it feels like that painting's watching."

Poppy nodded. "I know." She hopped up on to the chair just beside the door, a wooden one for the guide to sit on. She just hoped no one else came by and caught them, that was all.

"Get back against the walls!" Emily hissed. "I can hear them coming."

Maya darted to the windows, pulling the wooden shutters over to shut out some of the brightness in the room. Only thin beams of sunlight poured in now, dancing like spotlights, and Poppy nodded gratefully as Maya pressed herself against the wall with the others.

"Don't be stupid, Elspeth." Ali sounded angry, and a little bit frightened. She'd never heard her sound frightened before, Poppy realised. Angry, but not scared, not even when Izzy had accidentally pulled her into a canal. Ali's voice had gone all thin and sharp. "It isn't real."

"It is!" Elspeth gasped. "I want to go home. We shouldn't have started any of it. I hate it!"

Emily nodded fiercely at Poppy, who shook out the scarf in the dimly lit doorway, letting it swirl and flicker like the ghost she'd seen dancing on the water in her dream.

Outside in the passageway, someone screamed, and then there was a scuffling, and racing feet, and Ali and the others were gone.

SEVEN

"I'm really nervous now," Poppy muttered as Mr Finlay shepherded his pupils across the grass towards a big white tent. "The ghost story was stopping me being nervous, but now I think I might be sick."

"You won't," Emily told her. "Mrs Angel would kill you."

"Now I feel worse!" Poppy hissed.

"Oh look, there's Ali. Wow, look at Elspeth," Izzy muttered. "I think she actually has been sick. She's gone a really weird colour."

Poppy glanced sideways. Elspeth looked terrible – greyish white, with red eyes. She felt guilty for a minute, and then remembered the shadow spell. "It's her own fault," she muttered.

"It is," Izzy said firmly. "They shouldn't have done it to you first. About time someone got their own back, I say."

Poppy nodded. Ali had bullied Izzy for years. She'd done really horrible things to her, and Lucy and Elspeth had gone along with it. They deserved to be miserable for a bit. *And it probably won't last*, she added to herself with a sigh.

"Come on, Poppy. You have to be up at the front with the other designers." Mr Finlay hustled her forward, and Poppy just had time to make a panicked face at Izzy and the others.

There was a small group of children up at the front, definitely neater-looking than most of the others, as though the staff who came with them had made them tidy themselves up for the announcement. Poppy's mum had made her put on her nicest school skirt and the least paint-stained of her jumpers this morning, but some of these children looked as though they'd just been ironed. Poppy smoothed her skirt down and tried not to feel scruffy, and then giggled to herself. It probably wasn't helpful for a garden designer to be neat. They ought to have muddy fingernails, and leaves all over their clothes. Besides, Cam Morris looked a lot scruffier than she did, Poppy realised, as he bounded on to the little platform. The knees of his jeans actually *were* muddy. They'd seen him in the distance while they were eating their lunch, and he'd been crouching down to look at something in one of the flowerbeds. He'd probably started off the day neat and tidy for the ceremony too...

"Hello, all of you!" Cam Morris strode up and down the platform enthusiastically as he talked, and some of the girls closest squashed themselves back towards Poppy. He did look as though he was going to fall off if he wasn't careful. "This is such an exciting day! Today we get to find out which one of the wonderful schools we're going to be working with to build a fantastic new school garden. There were some brilliant designs. I'd like to build all of them, they were so imaginative. But we have to pick just one from this area. So – are you ready for the big announcement?"

Everyone cheered, and he beamed down at them.

"OK! I've got an envelope, somewhere..." He started to pat his pockets, until a patient-looking young man handed the envelope up to him. "Thanks! Yes – our winner is – Poppy Martin from Park Road School in Millford!"

Poppy had been so convinced that she wouldn't win – and so much more worried about Ali and spells and ghosts anyway – that she stared up at Cam Morris in disbelief, and didn't move.

"Poppy?" Cam Morris looked down at the group below him hopefully, and the other children glanced over their shoulders, wondering where she was. One of the smallest, tidiest girls was obviously about to burst into tears.

Poppy went pink and edged her way to the front. "I'm here," she said nervously.

"Excellent!" Cam Morris bounded over to shake her hand and pull her up the stairs on to the platform, and Poppy gulped as she saw her design appear on the screen at the back.

"Poppy's design is really original – elements of a medieval herb garden, combined with a modern sensory garden. And lots of brilliant ideas about using produce from the garden for school meals, plus some fantastic wildlife-friendly bits too. I'm amazed you managed to fit it all in, Poppy! And it still looks like a beautiful design! Really well done. You've obviously got a wonderful imagination."

Poppy smiled down at her feet, remembering the Green Lady. Perhaps she did have rather a good imagination, actually…

"So they're going to start building it next week?" Izzy's dad asked, looking interested. "Wow, they're moving fast. It's a nice time to start though, April. You'll be able to put vegetable plants out soon, and you'll have it looking great through the summer."

"They want to film all the gardens being made so that they can start to show the series on TV in September," Poppy said rather shyly – she didn't want to sound as though she was showing off. She and Mr Finlay had been given all sorts of information after the ceremony. Even Mr Finlay had looked a bit overwhelmed by it all. "The garden designer from *Growing Up* is coming to school tomorrow to look at the place where the garden's going to be. And then they're going to send a team of people with diggers and things in over the weekend. Mrs Angel had to send in a photo of the site with the design, you see. So they know what they've got to do to it."

"I suppose they've got to get rid of all the tarmac," Izzy said, nodding. The Year Six classrooms had been built on to the original school, and only that strange little bit of playground had been left round the edge.

Poppy nodded. It was hard to believe it was going to happen – that people were coming to tear up part of the playground, all because of her. And that her garden was going to be real…

"Mr Finlay?" Poppy looked at their teacher hopefully. Sometimes it was hard to tell if he was going to agree to something or not. "When the garden designer comes this afternoon, can Izzy come and help me talk to her as well?"

Mr Finlay looked surprised. "Why, Poppy? You're not usually shy. In fact, Izzy's usually the one who finds it hard to talk to people."

"It isn't that…" Poppy nibbled her bottom lip. She didn't want to explain about Ali's teasing, and the way she'd given up on her design way back at the beginning. For a start, it made her feel really stupid thinking about it now – she couldn't believe she'd let Ali push her around like that. But also because the Green Lady trick seemed to have really got to the three girls. Lucy looked pale and Elspeth hadn't even come to school today. Ali looked twitchy, and when George banged the door of the books cupboard, Poppy had seen her jump and shoot back in her chair, her eyes really wide and dark.

"Izzy persuaded me the design was good," she explained. "I wasn't going to send it in. I even threw it away! She took it out of the bin, and it had juice and chocolate all over it, so she and Maya and Emily tried to copy it out for me."

Mr Finlay stared at her. "Why didn't you think it was any good?" he asked, sounding shocked.

Poppy shrugged. "I don't really know a lot about gardens," she explained. "Izzy told me some of the wildlife ideas too, when we were talking about it in class. And her dad showed me some books."

Mr Finlay smiled. "You're a good team, all four of you. I should think it's OK if Izzy helps. You do realise they're going to film this, don't you?" he added.

"What?" Poppy squeaked, quite loudly. "They're filming today?"

Half the class stopped what they were meant to be doing, which was a very boring set of reading comprehension questions, and stared at Poppy and Mr Finlay. They'd known that Poppy had won, of course – lots of them had been at the ceremony. But no one had realised quite what this meant. Everyone had assumed the gardens were being built in the summer sometime.

Even Ali looked less wide-eyed and worried at the thought of being on television. There was about five seconds of silence, and then everyone started talking all at once.

"Oooh!"

"Oooh, sir, can we be in it?"

"Can we *all* be in it?"

"Will they come and film our class?"

Mr Finlay held up his hands in a pretend panic. "I don't know! Honestly, I don't. The designers are going to talk to Poppy, and that's all I've been told. I should think they'll want to film a bit of the school, just to show everyone what it's like. And they must be going to show the garden site, before they come and dig it all up. Before and after, that sort of thing."

Poppy hurried back to her seat, feeling a bit embarrassed. Of course she was excited about the filming, but she had a horrible feeling that everyone in the class was going to start fussing about it, and asking her if they could be in the programme. No one was going to believe that it wasn't up to her – but it wasn't. Joe, the patient-looking man who'd handed Cam Morris the envelope the day before, was part of the production team, and it was quite obvious that he was in charge, much more than Cam Morris, even if Cam was the star.

Luckily, before Poppy's entire class could spend break badgering her about getting them on TV, the crew arrived early and proceeded to get massively in the way. They did want to film the whole class, which was what everybody wanted, but that meant getting cameras and microphones in, and moving all the furniture round about six different ways. It was lunchtime before they were happy with it, and then the filming had to be done straight away before the light changed, which meant everyone was starving.

"At least we'll be on TV for a little bit," Emily said as they hurried up to the dining hall. "They said all of us would be, didn't they?"

"Yes!" said Poppy, rather grumpily. She was hungry, and she'd been made to have a conversation with Mr Finlay about numeracy (which didn't even make sense, as far as she could see) over and over again, while the film crew tried to get the sound levels right. She had stopped being excited about being on TV after about the fourth time. At least she had a packed lunch. Maya and Izzy were having school lunches, and they'd be lucky to get any.

"Was there anything left?" she asked as they came back to the table looking resigned.

"Mushrooms..." Izzy sighed. "I hate mushrooms. But there wasn't anything else."

"It can't be just mushrooms," Poppy said, peering at the greyish gloop.

"I don't want to know what else it is," Izzy said

sadly, stirring it with her fork.

"It's the veggie option," Maya pointed out. "This is what I get every day! Well, except I don't, because I almost always have a packed lunch. It was only that I fancied having a jacket potato today." She dribbled the grey gloop off her fork and stared at it. "We should make that production man eat this. Then he'd see what he'd done. I bet they've got a catering van as well. And the food will be gorgeous."

"A catering van?" Izzy frowned. "Like a kebab van?"

Maya shrugged. "Sort of. Except not with disgusting burgers made out of the bits of animals nobody even wants to think about. Nice food." She pushed the mushrooms away. "Want some bread, Izzy? There was a bit left. And some beetroot chunks on the salad bar."

"Yay, I can have a beetroot sandwich."

Poppy pushed her lunch towards Izzy to share, and Emily did the same as Maya came back with a handful of bread.

"I hope the vegetarian option becomes edible when we've got your garden," Maya said as she took a huge bite of bread.

"This is Lily – she's our garden designer."

"Ummm…" Izzy was so nervous about putting her hand up. But she was determined to stick up for Poppy's design. They'd gone through enough just getting it into the competition. She wasn't going to let anybody mess it around. "I thought Poppy was the designer," she said, looking apologetically at Lily.

"Don't panic," Lily told her cheerfully. "All I'm supposed to do is make sure the designs actually *work*. Yours is pretty sensible, Poppy, but one of the other winning designs has got a floating model cloud in the middle of it. I haven't worked out what I'm doing about that one yet."

"We may have to change some things," Joe pointed out. "But we'll try not to."

"I think these mosaic paths are great." Lily had a blown-up version of Poppy's design spread out over the table.

Poppy beamed at Lily. "I was hoping we could make them out of old plates, or something like that," she explained. "I was thinking everyone in the school could bring a manky old chipped plate in, and we could smash them, and then make the paths out of the bits! Otherwise people would just throw them away, wouldn't they?"

Lily was nodding delightedly, but Joe closed his eyes for a moment, looking slightly horrified. "Yesss … except that might be a slight health and safety problem."

"We could wear swimming goggles," Izzy suggested hopefully. She loved the idea of smashing plates. She might even be able to convince Dad to get rid of all the Peter Rabbit plates they'd had since she was a baby! She had to hide them before anyone came round, so he didn't serve up tea on them.

"I'm sure we can get round the safety issues," Lily murmured, scribbling notes. "This garden's full of nice recycled bits. And you've got lots of great ideas for gardening responsibly. All these water butts, and the wildflower patch."

"Do you think we can make the sculpture?" Poppy asked hopefully. "It's one of my favourite ideas. We found loads of bits of an old bike when we did a canal clean-up a few weeks ago. We put it all in a skip and got rid of it, but I kept thinking about how good some of the pieces looked – like they were artwork." She frowned. "I wish we'd kept them, but my mum would have been furious if I'd put lots of bits of rusty bike in my bedroom."

Poppy had added the sculpture as part of the Sight

section of the garden – she'd thought about putting a scarecrow in and then decided that actually she'd rather have a scare*boy* instead. She was pretty sure that lots of the flowers and vegetables were going to get ruined by people kicking footballs into them or racing round the different beds. So she'd designed her sculpture, a massive bird standing in the middle of one of the beds.

Izzy laughed. "I love his legs. You could grow beans up them or something."

"Ooooh, good idea." Lily nodded and scribbled harder. "I like the way you've got vegetables and fruit scattered through the garden actually, Poppy. It's not just in the Taste bit. Gives you a lot more room to grow things, as well."

Poppy looked round worriedly at the grim corner of the playground. This was the first time the production team had seen the place they were going to transform – apart from in photos. It looked awful – just tarmac, and one lone bench, and then a high brick wall that divided the school from the houses next door. It didn't look like it could ever be a garden. She glanced up at Joe and Lily anxiously, hoping they weren't going to be horrified.

But Lily was turning round slowly, looking up at the sky and squinting at the sun. "Mmmm… We might want to move your Taste bed, Poppy. You've got a nice bit of south-facing ground here. That means it'll be sunny," she added, as Poppy looked bewildered.

"Oh!" Poppy nodded. "I didn't even think about that," she said apologetically. "Is anything else in the wrong place?"

Lily was holding the plans out and pacing round the patch of ground. "I don't think so. Because we're starting from scratch, there's not as much worrying about what you've already got as there usually would be. It's fun – like a blank canvas!"

Poppy gave Izzy a relieved sort of smile. A blank canvas sounded exciting – as though they were painting the garden on to the crumbling tarmac.

Actually… A totally evil, very funny idea flitted into Poppy's mind. Her smile broadened into a grin, and she beamed into the camera. "Do you think we could have a mural as well?"

EIGHT

"That's mean," Izzy sniggered, and Poppy nodded. They were in PE, the last lesson of the day, and they were supposed to be planning a dance routine, but this was the first chance she'd had to tell the others about her idea.

"I know. Do you think it's *too* mean?"

"Of course not!" Izzy shook her head. "They definitely deserve it."

"We have to do it," Maya agreed. "Can we all paint a bit of it?"

Poppy nodded. "They're going to do most of the building of the garden at the weekends, and at the beginning of the Easter holidays – they said it would make too much mess and disturb everybody if they did it in term-time. But you can all come and help! There's a letter going out this afternoon." Poppy hurriedly arranged her arms into a vaguely dance-y sort of position, as she saw Miss Grace looking their way. "We'd better get on with making this dance up. Miss Grace is definitely watching us." She smiled to herself, glancing at Ali and Lucy, who were bossing Lara and Sophy around in the other corner of the hall. She would go home and draw her mural design tonight.

"Do you think they've worked out it was us yet?" Izzy asked her as they got changed after the class.

Poppy pulled her cardigan on, frowning. "I don't know. Ali hasn't said anything to me at all today, and she usually manages to get some nasty little comments in, doesn't she? She's definitely avoiding us."

Izzy nodded, and Emily sighed happily. "Best revenge ever. They really believe you called up a ghost."

Poppy smirked. "I think they do. And we're going to make sure they remember her every day…"

When she got home from after-school club, Poppy sat down at the kitchen table with a pad and her favourite pencils, so she could tell her mum and dad about the filming and what Lily had said about her design.

"They said we could put a mural in as well," Poppy

explained. "We've got big walls all round the garden, so we can paint all of them! It's a huge job," she said happily.

"Is that what you're drawing now?" her dad asked.

"Mm-hm. I want it to look like the garden goes on for much further than it really does, so I thought the mural could be mostly trees."

"Nice," her mum commented. "So it'll look green even in winter as well."

Poppy nodded, sketching branches and dabbling a haze of leaves over the top with her favourite watercolour pencils. Then she closed her eyes for a moment, remembering, and began to draw a slim figure in a flowing green dress, half hidden behind the trees. She added swirling brown-gold hair, dark, dark eyes and the high arched eyebrows she remembered from the portrait, and then sat back and smiled at her design. She needed to draw out a few more panels – there was quite a lot of wall – but this was the important one. When she was done, she'd get Dad to let her use the scanner, and then she could email it to Lily, who needed to order the special outdoor paint.

Ali and Elspeth and Lucy weren't going to forget the Green Lady in a hurry.

Poppy and Izzy sat on either side of the little path that wound past the raised beds, carefully pressing broken china pieces into the cement. It had turned out that even with everyone in the school bringing in battered plates, they didn't have enough for all the paths – mosaics took a lot more bits than Poppy had realised. But Lily had helpfully suggested making most of the paths in a mosaic of flat-topped pebbles, with just a ribbon of china bits running through them, and Poppy thought she was right. It would have been odd to have just one section of path covered in china pieces, and all the rest different. The really good thing was that the paths gave lots of people something to do. Almost everyone in the school had brought back the letters saying they wanted to help, even though it meant coming to school in the Easter holidays.

Poppy glanced up, looking round the garden. There were at least twenty people working on this path – they had to do it bit by bit or the cement dried before they got the pebbles in properly. And there were another fifteen or so painting the mural. Lily had drawn most of the outlines – Poppy had helped her a bit, but she wasn't tall enough to reach the tops of the walls without a ladder, which meant it took ages if she tried to do the trees. But she hadn't minded. She got to draw the more interesting bits at the bottom of the wall – rabbits, and a fantastic badger peering out between two trees that she was really pleased with. And, of course, the Green Lady. Once Lara and Sophy and a couple of other girls from their class had finished that bit of the trees, Poppy was going to paint her. She was really looking forward to it. And not just because she wanted to see Ali's face when she spotted the ghost.

Poppy had actually wondered whether Ali and the others would bother turning up this weekend, as she was pretty sure gardening wasn't their thing. But of course, they were desperate to be on TV. All three of them were over on the other side of the garden making a path, or rather, chatting and pretending to work until the cameraman happened to look their way.

Poppy went back to pressing the china pieces into the cement, a small smile twisting the side of her mouth – a smile like Sophia's in the picture. It was funny. She'd made up the whole story, and of course there never had been a ghost, but Poppy almost believed in her now too. She was sure that the floaty, shimmery figure behind the trees was going to make

111

the garden even more special. As though the Green Lady was going to watch over the garden. Poppy was sure that once she was painted into the mural, the garden would start to feel real, even though it didn't have any plants in it yet.

"Poppy, what's going here?" Lara called, pointing to the whitish patch where the Green Lady was waiting to be painted. "We're done with all the branches now, I think; there's just this bit left. It's going to be a person, isn't it? Who is she?"

Poppy got up and looked slowly along the wall. It wasn't perfect yet – there needed to be some plants, and the real fruit trees, to make the painted ones fit in. But already she could see that it was going to look brilliant.

"I can't believe you've done all those trees," she said happily to Lara and Sophy and the others. "Even the high bits. It looks amazing." Poppy ran her fingers over the Green Lady's bare face. "She's – she's like the spirit of the garden," she explained slowly. "I had a dream about her…" She glanced round at Lara, hoping that she didn't sound like a total fruit bat. She supposed most of the people in her class thought she was a bit mad anyway…

But Sophy only smiled, and traced a finger down

the outlines of the green dress. It was as though she understood the magic of the green girl too.

"Nice." Lara nodded. Then she looked hopefully at Poppy. "Poppy, you know we're going to do trees all round the garden? There's loads and loads of them. I don't mind painting them all, it's fun, but, well, can we add just one thing?"

Poppy blinked. "Oh! Did you want a horse in it? I can't draw them, Lara. I would, but they're so difficult. I always get the legs wrong. I'd ask Lily for you, but she's not here today."

"I can draw them!" Sophy said excitedly. "We both can. Horses are the only thing we *can* draw. Just one? A small horse, just a pony really. Peeping out round the trees?"

Poppy hugged her quickly. "Of course you can. You've been painting trees all day. What colour horse?" She giggled, remembering the pink unicorns in her fairy palace drawings. But Lara and Sophy weren't into pretty fantasy horses at all. They immediately went off into a very serious discussion about greys, and chestnuts, and which would look better in the wood, leaving Poppy to stand in front of the Green Lady, mixing just the right shade of paint.

"Poppy, just watch out for Ali, OK?" Izzy came up behind her and Poppy turned round, staring at her vaguely. She'd been painting the Green Lady for a while now, and she'd almost forgotten about the other people in the garden.

"What?" she murmured.

"Poppy! Wake up! Ali's seen what you're doing and she looks like she wants to strangle you right now! She'd probably even do it on camera."

"Izzy's right," Emily muttered as she and Maya hurried over to join them. "She's plotting something."

Poppy eyed her painting sadly. "I thought this might keep her off our backs for a while."

Emily shook her head. "I think the scare's worn off her. It was a couple of weeks ago, after all."

"She can only stop being mean for so long," Maya sighed. "I suppose the painting just reminds her of looking stupid."

Poppy shrugged. "I don't care. I love it. And I'm not changing it!" she added fiercely, glaring at the others.

"Calm down! No one said you should!" Emily rolled her eyes.

"It would be awful to change her," Maya said seriously. "All your paintings are amazing, Poppy, but

114

there's something special about this one. She's so …
mysterious."

"I know." Poppy stepped back off the wooden
edge of the raised bed, where she'd been balancing
to paint, and took a few more steps backwards to see
the whole wall properly. She shivered, her shoulders
twitching with excitement. Maybe it was just because
it was so *big* – but the wall looked fantastic.

"Wow, Poppy! That's really beautiful." Joe, the
producer, came bounding over. "We need to get you
standing right there for your piece to camera, I think.
It'll look great."

"Piece to camera?" Poppy repeated, looking at him
worriedly. No one had mentioned anything about
that.

"Yes, just a short piece. About your ideas for the
garden, how you're feeling about seeing it built. That
sort of thing." He grinned at her. "That's all right,
isn't it? You'll be fine. Let's get that set up for later on
this afternoon, shall we? After lunch?" And he shot
off again to organise somebody else.

"I don't want to do a piece to camera!" Poppy
wailed as soon as he was out of earshot. "Nobody
said I had to talk about the garden! I just wanted to
draw it!"

Maya burst out laughing and Poppy scowled at her. "It isn't funny!"

"Yes, it is! Everyone else is desperate to get on camera and have a starring part in the TV programme, and you hate it!"

Poppy sighed. "You could pretend to be me…"

"Why don't you want to?" Maya asked curiously.

"I don't know. I suppose Mum and Dad would love it. I'm just not very good at explaining stuff I draw." Poppy shook her head. "I'll sound stupid."

"Not as stupid as Cam Morris," Emily said, shaking her head, and the others stared at her. "Oh, come on! He sounds mad half the time, the way he talks! Really, Poppy, compared to him everyone's going to think you're a genius."

"My dad really likes his programmes," Izzy said, sounding a bit put out.

"So? He still sounds a total prat when he's going on and on. Like at Amberlake, when he was chuntering about gardens 'lifting our lives out of the everyday'. It didn't even make sense!"

Izzy sniggered. "I suppose so."

"Exactly." Emily nodded triumphantly. "Just don't talk rubbish about how plants speak to your heart, Poppy, and you'll be fine."

Poppy stood in front of the painted wall, trying not to look as nervous as she felt. She couldn't remember *any* of the stuff she was supposed to say.

"Are you all right, Poppy?" Mr Finlay asked her. "You're a bit pale."

"Just nervous," Poppy said apologetically. "I keep forgetting my words. And I wish they'd hurry up. They keep fiddling about with the microphone and it makes me nervouser."

"Sorry!" Joe called. "Bit of a problem with the sound. Give us a minute!"

Mr Finlay smiled. "You'll be fine, Poppy. Just tell them all the stuff you told me, about the different parts of the garden, and how you wanted it to be a place where everyone could see how amazing the world was, and how we had to look after it."

Poppy nodded doubtfully. As long as she didn't sound crazy, like Cam Morris. Mr Finlay hurried off to stop some of the boys throwing soil at each other, and Poppy stuck her hands in her hoodie pockets, trying to think of a way to make her garden sound interesting instead of mad. She wished she could have Izzy and Maya and Emily with her but the production team had shooed everyone out of the way. She was on her own.

"Poppy."

Poppy glanced round and jumped back, almost falling into the raised bed. Ali was standing next to her, smiling. She looked poisonous.

"What?" Poppy asked, hating the way her voice wobbled.

"I wanted to say I'm sorry." Ali nodded earnestly. "I shouldn't have said you cheated. I know you didn't. Well done. I know your design was the best."

Poppy stared at her. She didn't believe a word of it.

"And all the spell stuff – we shouldn't have done that. And I can see why you thought it would be fun to scare us with your ghost story." Ali smiled tightly.

Poppy looked at her nervously. What was all this about?

"So I brought you some chocolate. To say sorry." Ali was smiling hugely now, showing her perfect little teeth. She stuffed something into Poppy's pocket, and Poppy flinched.

"Um. Thanks... I can't eat it now. The filming – I have to talk."

Ali's mouth twisted crossly for a second, and then she was back smiling again. "Oh, sure. Don't worry. Have it later." And she slid away again, as quickly as she'd come.

"Ready, Poppy?" Joe called, and Poppy nodded doubtfully, trying to forget the weirdness of Ali and concentrate on what she had to say.

"OK. Now, don't worry. Remember we can edit this, so if you say something wrong, just pause and then start again. But try to smile!"

Poppy smiled tightly and started to talk, hoping the words she needed would appear somehow. It helped having her Green Lady behind her.

"Hi, I'm Poppy, and I'm from Park Road School in Millford. We're building a sensory garden, which I designed. It's a bit like a medieval herb garden – that's where I got some of my first ideas. But also I wanted it to be a garden that made people remember our planet and how amazing it is, and how we have to look after it…"

Poppy swallowed anxiously. Was that all she was meant to say? Had she missed something out? Nerves fluttered in her tummy as she tried to remember, and she jammed her hands in her hoodie pockets to stop herself twisting them together. She was so panicky that her hands felt itchy.

"I – um – designed a mural, because I wanted the garden to look bigger than it really is," she added, pulling out one hand to wave at the wall behind her. Then she screamed. The itching wasn't nerves. There was a massive brown and grey spider sitting on the back of her hand.

Even though Poppy loved the idea of using spider's webs as a natural dressing for cuts, and she'd designed bug shelters for the garden, she didn't actually like spiders all that much. And even someone who positively loved spiders would scream if they happened to find a huge one on their hand. She shook it frantically, but the spider clung on.

"Poppy, your pocket!" Izzy yelled, darting round the cameraman and running towards her. "They're in your pocket!"

Poppy looked down in horror and saw other things climbing out of the pocket of her hoodie: other wriggly, leggy things. She screamed again, scrabbling madly at her zip with the other hand, and still trying to shake the spider off.

"It's OK, Poppy." Mr Finlay grabbed the spider – he actually just picked it up, Poppy saw, suddenly realising that he was the best teacher in the history of the world. He hurried away to the other end of the garden with it cupped in his hands.

Izzy was undoing Poppy's zip, and Maya and Emily

120

wrenched the hoodie off and then hugged her.

"Ali must have put them in my pocket," Poppy sobbed. "She said it was chocolate."

"That was Ali?" Mr Finlay snapped. Poppy hadn't seen him come back. "Ali Morgan, get over here now! And you, Elspeth. And Lucy. All of you."

"Oh, they're in big trouble," Emily said blissfully. "They're dead."

Poppy sat down shakily on the edge of the raised bed, and one of the crew handed her a bottle of water. She looked a bit shaky too.

"Are you OK?" she asked. "I can't stand spiders, and that one was massive. I'd have run a mile."

"Do I have to do it all again?" Poppy whispered miserably, glancing up at Joe, who was crouching next to her, looking worried.

"Actually, what you said before the spider was great. We'll be fine with that. Wow, I'd forgotten how mean girls can be sometimes. You lot should go on over to the catering van and get yourselves some cake. That'll make you feel better. Honestly."

"You'll feel even better if you look at Mr Finlay yelling at Ali," Izzy whispered, nudging Poppy with her elbow.

"Oh, look." Maya gave a little sigh of delight. "That's just mean. Mr Finlay is amazing."

Poppy nodded fervently, remembering the spider. "Totally amazing. What's he done?" She was trying to eat a piece of lemon cake – Maya had been right, the catering van had yummy food, much, much better than school lunches – but it was mostly a pile of crumbs on her plate. It seemed to catch in her throat when she tried to swallow it. She craned her neck to see over Maya's shoulder – they were sitting on the edge of one of the new raised beds with their cake.

Mr Finlay was standing in the middle of the garden, with his arms full of bright-orange high-vis vests. A bit like the ones the girls had used when they were doing their canal clean-up.

"I didn't know we were supposed to wear those for the gardening," Poppy murmured.

Maya patted her shoulder gently. "We don't have to, Poppy. Wake up."

"Who's that with him?" Izzy asked curiously, and Poppy frowned. "That's Rachel. The one who did my make-up." She'd had to have some base and blusher before they filmed her, just to make sure she didn't looked washed out, Rachel had said. "What's she doing? Are they going to film Ali and Elspeth and Lucy?" Her mind was still half on the scratchy feeling of little spider feet, and she knew she was being slow.

"Yes, of course they are! And she's making them take all their make-up off!" Emily squeaked. "Oh, wow... No make-up, and bright-orange high-vis vests. They'll die if they have to be on TV like that. With millions and millions of people watching them. This is even better than the Green Lady. We need to get Mr Finlay a present."

Poppy smiled slowly, watching as Rachel stood in front of Ali with a packet of cotton wool pads, making her take off every last bit of mascara. Ali looked furious – and oddly pale and pink-eyed.

"She must wear mascara to school every day," Maya muttered. "I don't think I've ever seen her without make-up on. She's brilliant at getting it past the teachers."

Joe came by and winked at Poppy. "Don't worry, we'll make sure we get this bit in. Your little mates digging in their lovely orange outfits."

"Girls! Come down and see this!" Poppy's mum called. "You're in the paper!"

Poppy bounced up off her bed, and Maya, Emily

and Izzy raced downstairs after her. She'd begged Mum to let her have a sleepover for the last weekend of the Easter holidays. It wasn't her birthday or anything, but she felt like she wanted to say thank you to her friends for looking out for her over the last few weeks.

"Look!" Her mum spread the paper out on the kitchen table and the four of them huddled together to read it.

"Park Road School to star in new TV series!" Poppy read. "Well, one episode. Still, it's sort of true." There was a big photo of her standing in front of the Green Lady in the middle, and loads of other photos. Poppy shivered, realising she was wearing her hoodie – this must have been taken just before the spiders climbed out of her pocket. She hadn't worn that hoodie since.

"The production company must have given them these as stills," Maya said. "I didn't see anyone from the paper around."

"What are stills?" Emily whispered to Poppy, and Maya went pink.

"Sorry. Mum talks about all this kind of stuff. It's a photo taken while you're filming. You know. Still instead of moving."

"You look really nice, Poppy," Izzy said, reading the captions under all the photos. "And the mural looks amazing!"

"Oh, wow, I hadn't seen this one!" Emily burst out laughing and pointed to the picture in the corner. "Look at them!"

Ali was glaring out of the photo, looking furious. She had a streak of mud down one cheek, and the orange vest had turned her face a sickly sort of colour. Elspeth and Lucy just looked fed up.

"It's going to be great building the rest of the garden, and planting everything, but I really can't wait for September," Poppy said, giggling, as they went into the living room to watch a DVD. "It'll be like a proper garden by then, or almost. All the plants will have grown a bit and they won't just look like they've been shoved in."

Izzy nodded. "We'll even have had tomatoes and beans and things by then. Grown in our own garden! And then the TV series will be on."

Poppy smiled. "Yup. I can mute the part where I'm talking, but there's one bit that I really have to see…"

The four friends laughed. It was great to have something so amazing to look forward to, but first they had a sleepover to get on with!

If you enjoyed this book,
then you'll love

Dear Scarlett

by

FLEUR
HITCHCOCK

Turn the page for a sneak peek!

A Box

- - - - - - - - - - - -

Bing bong. The doorbell.

I listen, but nothing happens.

Bing bong. The doorbell again.

My baby brother, Syd, pauses. He's feeding dinosaurs to the laundry bin. He smiles and hands me a slimy stegosaurus.

Bing bong, bing bong, bing bong.

Rats. Mum must be deaf or something.

I lower myself from the top bunk, headfirst. I've got the sheet wrapped round my waist. It's how I'd like to escape from a burning house, but this time all the bedding comes with me and I end up crashing to the floor.

Bing bong!

"Coming!" I yell. I pull on some jeans and peer out of the window. I can only just see through the glass because all the rain there ever was seems to be trying to fall on our house, and most of it's racing down my window. There's a battered half-timbered car wedged between the large concrete rectangles that make up the watercress beds at the back of our house. Mr Hammond, the watercress-bed man, is talking to whoever it is, pointing at our front door, but I can't actually see anybody.

I don't recognise the car and, for one second, I wonder if something exciting might be about to happen. Perhaps someone's come to tell me I've won something.

I drag on yesterday's dirty T-shirt, and try to remember if I ever did enter the Sugar Puffs "Honey Monster challenge" or whether the cardboard packet's still stuck behind the toaster. I'm pretty sure it's stuck behind the toaster.

Putting my hands on the banisters, and without using my feet, I slide over Syd's stair gate and arrive silently at the bottom of the stairs.

I look round for Mum. She's doing her morning

yoga with earplugs. She hasn't even heard the door.

I stop in the hallway, looking out.

Somebody's standing on the other side of the glass, pressing against it; but because our front door's made of this ancient cloudy glass with little ships on, I can only see a shadow. I'm guessing they don't have an umbrella and they're trying to get out of the rain.

Bing bong.

For a moment I wonder if it's a mad axe murderer, but then decide that mad axe murderers probably never call at nine o'clock on a Saturday morning.

I look again at the shadow. I don't think it's a scary shadow, it's really no taller than I am.

I'll take a chance.

I yank open the front door.

"Scarlett? Scarlett McNally?" It's a round shiny man in a sheepskin jacket, with a Father Christmas beard. He is definitely not a mad axe murderer but he doesn't look like he's come to tell me I've won anything. He looks more like someone buying watercress. I'm sure people who tell you you've won something drive cars that were built this century. He's holding a box.

"Yes?" I say, looking round at Mum, who's

stretching now. She still hasn't noticed anything but I expect I can handle this.

"Morning, Scarlett. I was your father's solicitor." He's standing right in the doorway now; half of his jacket's dark with the rain.

Solicitor?

I don't know what to say, so I stare at the man. I go on staring at him. I can stare at people for ages, and they can never do it back anything like as well. It gives me the upper hand. I can see he's getting uncomfortable, so I give him a chance and blink.

He's looking really confused now. "I'm acting on your father's instructions."

"Dad's – but he's…"

"Yes, Scarlett, but he left these items in my care, to be given to you on, or around, your eleventh birthday. You were eleven last week, weren't you?" He grips the box as if he's about to whisk it away.

"Yes – Tuesday."

"Well, happy birthday last Tuesday. It's yours now." He plonks the box on the carpet, fumbles for the door handle, touches his hat and trips out through the door.

"Why did I have to be eleven?" I ask, calling into the rain.

"Haven't a clue – perhaps he thought you'd be old enough to avoid some of his less lovely friends?" He scuttles back to his car, his shoulders hunched against the rain. "Don't get too excited." The door squeaks as he clambers in and when he closes it, a small piece of wood pings off the side.

Reversing, he narrowly misses one of the watercress beds and lurches off through some puddles. The battered car swings out on to the main road and disappears.

I stare at the box, then I pick it up and shake it. It rattles, but only a little.

Dad.

It's from my dad.

My dad the burglar. My dad the thief. The person that no one mentions.

He's been dead for five years.

Ellie and
Uncle Derek

I sit at the bottom of the stairs, staring at Mum's back through the doorway of the living room. I almost call her, but then I look at my name written on top of the box, and I don't.

I could always tell her later.

I can hear Syd dropping cars into the bath. They sound really loud.

Perhaps I *should* tell Mum. She'll be cross that I didn't tell her straight away, but then she'll be weird and moody if I tell her now.

She's funny about dads. She's funny about my dad in particular.

Anyway, it's got my name on it. Not hers.

I pick up the box and carry it up the stairs, to sit on my bed. It fits comfortably on my knees.

The brown parcel tape across the top has one corner that's not quite stuck down.

I wish the man *had* come from Sugar Puffs; this feels like it's going to be complicated. I don't know a lot about Dad, I'm not sure I want to know a lot about Dad, but I'm tingly, my whole body's fizzy. It's as if my blood's turned into fizzy water.

I can't work out if I'm excited, or scared.

Dad?

This came from Dad?

I tug at the tape.

The cardboard flaps spring open, pushed by a mass of balled-up newspaper.

I jump, breathe deeply and straighten out a sheet of newspaper. It's old, but it doesn't say anything special. I feel a slight pang, a dulling. The fizz feels less like tonic water and more like flat cola. But I reach my hand inside.

It closes around something soft, maybe suede? There's metal inside, it clanks. A jewellery case? Perhaps it's a velvet purse full of gold rings and emerald necklaces? Some booty from a long-forgotten heist. I pull it out and run my fingers over it with my eyes closed. No, not jewellery, but a case, holding something metal.

It could still be precious.

I open my eyes. It's brown and oily, not at all like a jewellery case. A leather roll, tied with two long straps. I fumble to undo them, and it tumbles from my hand, falling open across the floor.

Tools?

TOOLS?!?

Just a load of long thin scratchy tools; not a screwdriver in sight.

A lot of rude words go through my head and then I remember what they are.

They're picklocks.

I've seen them before. I close my eyes and I'm back, tiny, so small I can just see over the side of Mum's patchwork quilt. Mum's there, sitting on the bed; she's doing something, maybe brushing her hair?

Dad's there too, his long fingers wrapping the tools, slipping the leather strap around the outside and buckling it closed. I can smell him, something he puts on his hair, or is it his jacket? It's warm and musky.

He picks me up and throws me so I land on the bed and the laughter bursts up from my chest and I reach out for more, but he's leaving again, like he always does.

He smiles at me, his eyes creased and blue and bright before vanishing through the bedroom door. The memory hovers at the side of my head.

The tools feel really big and heavy in my hand, like something that's waiting to be mentioned, something that only grown-ups have, but I know Mum won't like them and she'll take them away from me, so I slip them under the bed.

I reach back into the box and grope about. My fingers pass over some thin bundles of shiny card wrapped in elastic bands, but I grab the largest thing I can find.

Gone with the Wind.

I know this book, it's about a stroppy girl called Scarlett O'Hara. My namesake.

Why on earth would Dad give me that? There's already a copy here, one he gave Mum when I was born.

I reach back into the box and pull out two bundles of photos and postcards.

I peel off the elastic bands. There's one of Mum

looking really young and gorgeous and another of someone who I think is probably Dad, looking sharp. Sideburns and pointy shoes. Some people I don't recognise; some places I've never been to.

The tingly feeling's almost gone away now. There was no golden necklace or emerald ring. I'm back on my bedroom floor with the sound of Syd's cars clanging into the bath.

All I've got is a pile of pictures and a set of tools.

Bing bong.

Maybe the man's back to tell me I *have* won the Sugar Puffs challenge.

I stuff the box under my bed. Syd's on the landing with his arms out, so I pick him up and stumble past the stair gate, letting him clamber backwards down the stairs.

I open the front door.

It's Uncle Derek and Ellie.

Rats. I'd forgotten about Ellie. She's coming to sleep over so that Mum and Uncle Derek can both get to work today. He's on duty now, and Mum's cooking in the care home this evening. Ellie's clutching a big pink flowery duvet, and a white fluffy bear. "Hi, Scarlett," she says.

She's got this drippy voice that always ends on a

low note and she draws smiley faces over her "i"s. I almost can't stand her, but then, nor can anyone else.

"Hi, Ellie. Hi, Uncle Derek," I say, letting them in, forcing myself to smile.

"Morning, Scarlett," says Uncle Derek.

"Oh," calls Mum from the kitchen. "Derek!"

She comes out of the kitchen, wiping her hands on her leggings. She stops in the hall and Uncle Derek pecks her on the cheek. She goes red.

So does he.

He's not really my uncle.

"Oh, Carole, thanks so much, just off to see the new CCTV set-up, in the council offices, yes…" Uncle Derek rubs his chin and twitches in the doorway. He can't stay still. He's a plain-clothes policeman and likes running marathons. I expect he'll run to work today through all the puddles, and then catch a criminal or two and run back with them under his arm. "So, I'll be back at five-fifteen, all right?"

Mum smiles and picks up Syd.

Ellie and I stare at them.

They don't notice us.